THE GATHERING

THE GATHERING

A Mystery
by
Elisabeth Pollack

North Country Press • Unity, Maine

Cover design By Write Angle Communications, Camden, Maine
Cover art by Maureen Hunter, Unity, Maine
Printed in the United States by J.S. McCarthy, Augusta, Maine

ISBN Hard Cover 0-945980-60-4
         Trade Paper 0-945980-63-9

Library of Congress Cataloging number 96-70110

For Mike and Ian Pollack
of British Columbia.

Acknowledgements

Thanks to Bob Bahre, Anne Gass, "Skip" Herrick, and Milton Mills

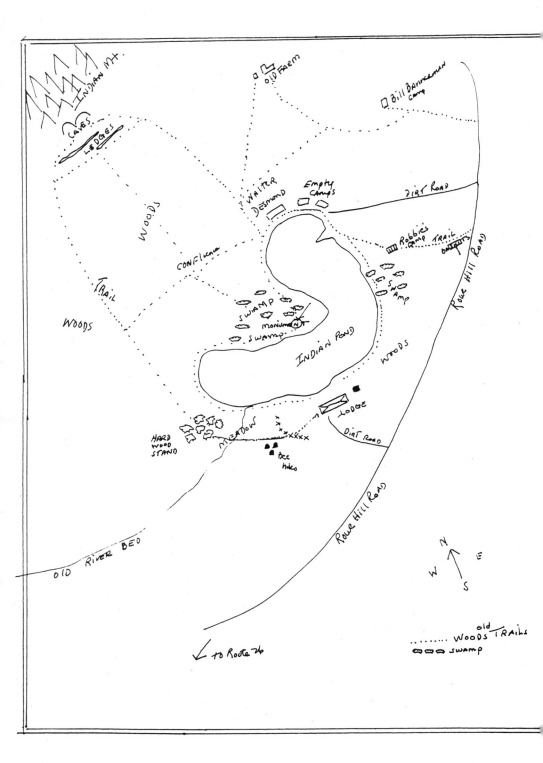

CHARACTERS

Lee Heaward	A real estate broker in Paris, Maine.
Hod Cole	Lee's friend. A Maine woodsman who likes to solve puzzles.

Leading characters of *The Rowantree Crop*, the first book of the series.

A.E. Gibbons	Owner of Indian Lodge in the Bryant Pond area.
Motorboat Jones	A trucker.
Enough Peabody	Yard boy at Indian Lodge. Motorboat's ward.
Peggy Canevari	Waitress and all-around helper at Indian Lodge.
Walter Desmond	Head of Indian Mountain Bank in Bethel.
Carol Desmond	Walter's wife.
Dick Eggleston	State trooper.
Freida Eggleston	Dick's pregnant wife.
Bill Bannerman	Retired teacher who summers in Maine.
Alexander Fremont	Retired minister interested in Maine Indians.
Dr. Anna Easton	Area doctor and medical examiner.
Robbie Moulton	A basketmaker. Last of the Swampers.
Richard Wortham, Jr.	A newspaper reporter.
Debbie & Chuck Sherman	Guests at Indian Lodge.

Various deputies, searchers, and guests. And Kate, Lee's Gordon Setter.

PROLOGUE

Lee Heaward had been following the horse trailer ever since she had left the turnpike entrance at Gray. Dusk was closing in as she drove Route 26 north toward South Paris and High Meadows Farm. She was weary in mind and body from the past week spent in Connecticut with an old friend who was dying. It had been a week of saying goodbye, doing what friends do for each other. There was a haven at High Meadows, and Lee visualized the fireplace and a cup of tea at the end of her journey. More important, Hod.

Lee sighed. She was anxious to drive the last few miles, but the horse trailer ahead of her kept speeding up and slowing down. Passing was impossible, a single line of cars now followed the trailer, and with darkness falling, she had to check her impatience with the driver. No sense taking a chance.

Something disturbed Lee about the horse trailer. She had noticed it at Gray when she drew up behind it at the ticket window as they left the turnpike. It was loaded on the wrong side. First she had thought it carried two horses, but now she could see that it held only one, on the right-hand side.

That fellow, she said to herself, doesn't know much about loading trailers. He'll have an accident if he isn't careful.

If you had one horse, you'd load on the left. If you were stupid and couldn't remember that, just connect two L's — load and left. Never one horse on the right. It tended to pull the hauler over and could cause trouble. Rarely did you see a mistake. If you had a trailer, chances were you understood trailering. As a matter of fact, thought Lee as she again looked for a spot to pass, this fellow can't know horses very well. She noted the Massachusetts plates and wondered who was hauling a horse all the way to Maine loaded on the wrong side.

Just then a spot opened, a long stretch of oncoming road with no cars in sight, and Lee pulled out and around. Busy with the road, the lights, and the oncoming dark, she saw very little of the outfit she passed other than that the trailer was dark blue and a jeep-type car pulling it looked like a Toyota. Then she was ahead, pulling into line, and she washed her mind of the trailer until two weeks later, when Hod and Dick Eggleston, the state trooper, walked back to the farm and came upon the Toyota and the trailer, stripped of their plates, hidden behind the barn. And no sign of either driver or horse.

Once again, Lee and KHod found themselves in murder.

CHAPTER ONE

Robbie's old green felt hat, banded with a red cord, came down so low over his eyes that when he looked at you the effect was one of a ferret peeking out his hole. This was of course, if he looked at you at all, for he tried to avoid any social intercourse and spent most of his days alone. Except for the times when people came to his shack to buy his baskets—baskets made the same way his mother had made them and her mother before her, baskets that were famous up and down the valley. Then Robbie would speak, in a curious, low, soft voice, stroking each word as if it were a sound wrapped carefully as a gift might be wrapped for a child on a special day. He would answer questions about the gathering baskets he was most noted for, sturdy ash baskets with swing handles that could carry heavy apples and potatoes as well as the lighter loads of herbs and flowers. Even then he would not talk at length to anyone.

There were two exceptions.— Lee Heaward and A.E. Gibbons.

On this late August day of cirrus clouds and faint breezes, weather signs usually forewarning a storm, Robbie was woods walking. He was looking for ash trees — black ash, sometimes called brown ash, would be best but this was scarce. Most basketmakers who cut their own bolts settled for white ash. He would cut in midwinter, or very early spring and drag the bolts home to store behind his shack. Later he would pound them into long, thin strips—these to be stored on the porch. The ash trees had to be straight and true without too many scarrings. Robbie's eyes flickered from side to side. He had been looking all morning for trees to mark for cutting next spring. He was now on A. E. Gibbons's land, behind his own. He had walked through the swamp at the end of Indian Pond and he was now halfway up Indian Mountain.

His pack basket was heavy. He was tired now and needed to rest. He remembered the ledges near the top of the mountain, those stone outcroppings running just below the cave openings. He halted a moment, resting on the stout applewood staff that gave him balance, and then, calculating his distance from the summit, he pushed forward. His feet were not in the moccasins one would have expected, but Nike walkers, well worn and stained with the walnut hulls he used to stain his baskets.

The August day was warmer than Robbie had expected. He opened the top button of his old flannel shirt and pushed up his sleeves. There were still woods flies and he did not want to strip down entirely. He sighed. The pack basket seemed heavier than usual and he rubbed his shoulders as his eyes searched out the turn in the trail that would lead up to the ledges. Fir grew heavily in this area—black growth, the timbermen called it. Underfoot was princess pine and club moss, and he had seen a patch of pipsissewa a while back. He wondered if he had missed the turn.

But there it was. He swung up to the left and within another two minutes came out just below the first ledge, the outcropping that overlooked Indian Pond and the valley below.

Gratefully, he eased the pack basket from his sore shoulders and settled himself into a comfortable depression in the rock. It was a favorite place for Robbie. As a child he had come here often to soothe his feelings when other children had laughed at him.

Now I am King of the Mountain and Lord of all I survey.

Today, tired as his bones were, it was necessary to tell himself this truth again. He had to know he could still climb his mountain. He could not yet give in to his aching bones.

Far below him, barely audible, came the sound of a truck on Route 26. A faint breeze stirred the tops of the firs and the smaller hardwoods at the top of the mountain. Below, the long, narrow valley wove a tapestry in shades of green. Indian Pond, boomerang-shaped, shimmered gray-green. At the north end of the pond the swamp showed bronze and black as the waters narrowed and the bog began.

Robbie's eyes swept the valley and came to rest on the lawn in front of Indian Lodge. He could hear a lawn mower coughing as it started.

Enough. He must be going to mow the lawns.

Robbie leaned back wearily and closed his eyes. He slept and the mountain waited.

Inside Indian Lodge, in the shower stall of the small bathroom behind the first-floor stairs, where the door lock had never worked properly, A.E. Gibbons hurried to get in and out before she might be interrupted. The old-fashioned oak telephone, mounted on the wall outside the bathroom door, had been ringing all morning. A.E. had answered twice to take reservations for the following week. Peggy, the "helper-outer," had answered three times to book reservations in September, and Mr. Fremont himself, who was staying with them for the next three weeks on his usual jaunt to Maine, had asked her this morning at breakfast to be sure not to put him out just because Indian Lodge had suddenly been discovered by the outside world.

A.E. lathered her tall, thin body with a wild rose soap Peggy had given her for Christmas, rinsed the last of the shampoo out of her graying red hair, and grabbed a towel off the peg.

Whatever happened to my privacy? I should have had my head examined, talking to that reporter.

She pulled on worn jeans, thrust her arms through a clean yellow shirt, and twisted her hair into a tight roll, securing it at the top of her head with a tortoiseshell comb. She applied lipstick in the vicinity of her mouth—that should suffice. She gave the shower a swipe with the sponge, ran the suds down the drain, and left the bathroom, noting that the door lock really needed to be fixed this year.

I'm not sure I want this, not sure at all.

She strode down the hall into the kitchen, thoughts still milling about in her head.

I'm not sure I want to be discovered by the outside world. Things were just fine the way they were.

Only four months ago, in early May, Mr. Richard A. Wortham Jr., the travel editor of a New York paper, had lost his way in some inconceivable fashion. After all, how many roads are there in Oxford County? He had driven down the long, narrow, dirt road winding in from Rowe Hill to Indian Pond. It was mud season, and Mr. Richard A. Wortham Jr. hadn't a clue to the fact that his beautiful white Caddy, complete with white leather seat covers and a bar in the back, was going to sink halfway up to its wheel covers in the mud that made Indian Pond road passable only to four-wheel drives in late April and May. It had taken two hours and a tractor to pull him out, and by then he had taken refuge in the lodge with some of Peggy's muffins and English tea to soothe him. Hesitantly, A.E. had answered questions about the lodge, and Mr. Wortham, charmed with the old place and its owner, stayed the night.

He repaid the hospitality with a mention in his column, "New Discoveries in New England Inns." Since then Indian Lodge was fast becoming a success.

But A.E. was not happy. She had not realized the implications of notoriety.

Whatever happened to my privacy?

In the kitchen of the great old Adirondack-style building on this August morning, Peggy Canevari finished the breakfast dishes and attacked the long Monel-covered sink. Slate countertops stretched along one side of the room, and black-and-white tiled linoleum covered the floor. A 1930s square refrigerator, its door bound with stainless steel hinges, took up one corner of the room. The distance between range, sink, and refrigerator was far from present-day standards for an efficient workspace. Roller skates would have been helpful in this kitchen, and A.E. had once given the idea some thought, but she had abandoned it as being too frivolous.

Looking at it now, in light of the fact that maybe the lodge was poised on the brink of success, A.E. reconsidered.

"Peggy, I've made Mr. Fremont's bed and I did the pies this morning before you came. I'm going to see how Enough is doing with that lawn mower. I need a breath of air. I made a new schedule—it's there by the phone in case anyone else calls. Just fill in the days. Be sure to take phone numbers." She took an old sweater off the peg and headed out on the porch.

There was no whine of the mower, no sign of Enough. Where was that boy?

A.E. sighed and turned around to look at the lodge. Her lodge, her inheritance, her problem—a perfect specimen of Adirondack architecture hidden on the shore of this 100-acre pond. It was the only structure, save for three cottages on the north shore, reached by a different road than the narrow ribbon that wound almost half a mile from Rowe Hill Road through the woods to the lodge.

A small clientele of out-of-staters had passed the knowledge of this hidden place down through their families and added a few friends to the list. They came from June through October to enjoy fishing in the pond and the simple facilities of this late-1800s lodge. A few skiers had discovered the lodge through word of mouth—A.E. did no advertising. Slowly, a clientele had been built, unlike that of the condominiums and motels that serviced the area. Just enough to get by, but not enough to improve. For, if the truth was to be told, A.E. really didn't want to become a successful innkeeper. She much preferred to go fishing.

Mr. Richard J. Wortham, Jr. had different ideas—and A.E. hadn't had sense enough to keep quiet.

It serves you right. Now look what you got yourself into. You're going to have to fix the place up which means you're going to have to go to the bank and ask for money—workmen around and people booked all summer long and heaven knows how many in the winter. The road has to be plowed and sanded and maybe even tarred in the Spring. You're going to have to work harder and carry more insurance, and there won't even be time to go fishing. You're going to be a success and the whole world is going to beat a path to your door or the lodge's door. Is that what you want?

It would probably make Mr. Richard J. Wortham, Jr. very happy— another place for him to add to his list of inns you don't want to miss. But I'm not sure it's going to make me happy.

A.E. stood looking at the lodge, the thoughts threading slowly through her mind. The two-story log building had been built in the late 1800s, a long structure with its roofline interrupted by a tower at one end. A covered porch ran the entire length. Huge log pillars supported the porch roof, and granite steps led up at the front and on either end. From one of the old Roosevelt rocking chairs that marched in a row across the porch one could look the length of the pond to the boomerang bend. Indian Lodge sat in a natural pocket on one side of the southeast shore, a pocket that sloped gradually down to a small sand beach. From the west side of the lodge the lawn sloped away to an old garden spot where old-fashioned everblooming roses climbed over a snake fence and yellow marguerites and purple asters in long beds fought a losing battle against the grass. In the spring daffodils bloomed there. On this August day the roses scented the air and their yellow petals were a mecca for the bees that A.E. kept in two hives far back in the meadow. An opening in the snake fence led into the meadow, and a winding path led upward into a hardwood stand at the foot of Indian Mountain. Here the path wound up to the caves and the ledges where Robbie, lord of all he surveyed, sat sleeping.

The lawn mower started up again, and A.E., satisfied that Enough was back at work, decided to check on the supply of fireplace wood stacked behind the old barn to the north of the lodge. Finished with her inspection, she returned to the kitchen to pick up the list for town and decide whether she would call the bank. The hum of the mower faded, and A.E. knew that Enough by now was doing the outside perimeter of the large old croquet area.

Enough Peabody, weaving his rotary lawn mower to and fro across the lawn of Indian Lodge, was actually driving his souped-up stock car in the New Hampshire International Speedway races. He was rounding a curve right now, shifting up, and making a run the long length of the side by the stands, his helmeted head straining forward to watch the car ahead, his every thought on winning. It would be time for a pit stop and his crew would change tires and give him encouragement, and this time he would emerge the winner, the youngest driver ever in New Hampshire. This time, this time. Enough dreamed as he mowed, a fourteen-year-old whose head and feet never matched. Thoughts of his race mingled with the smells of a fresh-baked pie, and although he did not wear a watch, his inheritance from a long line of Indian ancestors set his time at eleven o'clock on this August morning. Time for a drink of water, and if he wandered inside, it was a sure thing either A.E. or Peggy would produce pie and milk. The lodge's owner was thoughtful of her help, generally willing to listen to Enough and his plans and agree with him that he wasn't going to push lawn mowers forever. This morning, perhaps, but not forever.

Rounding the last strip of the large lawn and cornering the perennial bed filled with both flowers and weeds, Enough's eyes caught motion far out in the meadow at the edge of the hardwood stand. Then the mower turned the corner, and he was out of range.

Probably the honeymooners. They had been making love all over the grounds since their arrival three days ago, and according to A.E., it was impossible to know where to step as they picked the most unlikely places.

Enough grinned. He had been trying for quite a few weeks now to entice Peggy into a corner of the meadow himself, but exactly how he was going to handle things when he got her there he was not yet sure. Motorboat had given him the facts of life at age five, but even now, at fourteen, Enough hadn't been faced with the necessity of remembering them.

Without Motorboat Jones, Enough's life would have been grim. Motorboat, given name Ellwood, had taken the boy from the beginning when five brothers and sisters had been too many for his mother to take care of. The Silvertown area held no future for Enough. Motorboat had simply helped his sister out, to use a Maine expression, and raised the boy as his own. Maverick that he was, Motorboat kept a neat house, saw that Enough was fed and clothed and taught him the things he should know even before his formal schooling began. Now a high school freshman, Enough spent his summers working at Indian Lodge, a job Motorboat had suggested and insisted Enough apply for himself.

The fact that Motorboat admired A.E. might have had something to do with it, but that was Motorboat's secret.

Enough brought his stock car to a screeching halt and sprinted up the steps to the screened kitchen door.

"Can I come in, A.E.? Guess I could use a drink of water."

"How about a piece of apple pie? With a glass of milk?

Or aren't you hungry?" A.E. smiled as she cut the fresh pie without waiting for an answer.

"Boy, could I! Motorboat says you make good pies, the best ever, he says." Enough slid into the old arrow backed Windsor chair at the end of the long harvest table.

"Motorboat says—"

"I know what he says." A.E. looked hard at Enough. "You better just eat your pie and go on back to your mowing. When you get finished, bring me in some carrots, will you ? And see if you can finish weeding that row of beets. There's another hour until lunchtime."

"O.K." Enough knew when the tall persimmony looking woman was not in a talking mood. He'd learned to gauge her responses. If she cut him off, it was time to leave her alone. He grinned at Peggy, who smiled back and with inner satisfaction, he finished his pie, corralling the last bit of buttery crust. "I'm out of here."

"Don't forget the carrots. I'm going to town right after noontime." A.E.put the pie back on the shelf of the old-fashioned iron cookstove and covered the dish with a round net cover she had found at an antique shop, one of three, hanging on the wall behind the stove-they looked like the breastplates of Amazon maidens. A.E. had been tempted to tell him just that when Mr. Robert J. Wortham, Jr. had asked her what in the world those things were.

Enough went back to finish mowing and pulling carrots. A.E. went to her desk in her third-floor tower room to struggle with her checkbook and decide how much she could realistically ask for at the bank. Peggy mopped the kitchen floor without enthusiasm, and up on the ledges, far above the lodge, Robbie snoozed in the noonday sun.

Enough finished, deposited the carrots in the kitchen sink, gave Peggy a swift left-handed squeeze, and, taking his brown paper bag in hand, gave thought to where he would eat his lunch. It was true that any day he wanted he could have lunch in the kitchen, for A.E. had offered it at the beginning of his employment, but he wanted this hour to himself. Although he looked forward to the snacks in between, he brown-bagged lunch nearly every day in the summer.

Today he decided on the hardwood stand. A.E. had spoken last week of possible work there in the early fall after school hours. There was a small amount of blowdown, and if Enough used a chain saw, he could clear it away and chunk it up in proper sizes for the parlor woodstove and the big fireplace. He would haul it along the path through the meadow to the barn to be stored for the winter. A.E. liked a fair amount put up on the long porch, too. She said it gave her a sense of well being in case the snow was heavy. The old kitchen woodbox and the parlor wood chest only held one day's supply. Having wood in one corner of the porch made A.E. feel safe. She liked wood heat. She liked to save on oil, and if there was one thing Amelia Earhart Gibbons was, she was a saving woman.

Enough followed the path past the perennial bed, past
the bee-laden yellow roses, into the meadow. The brown paper bag scribed circles in the air. He would give himself half his lunch hour for eating and half for looking. Then he'd return to the house and ask A.E. what she wanted done for the rest of the day. He knew she was planning on going into Bethel. If he was lucky she'd be gone, and he could hang out for a couple of hours teasing Peggy. He wasn't a stock car racer for nothing.

Motorboat, who ran a garage and trucking business, had taught Enough to divide days into blocks of time, not doing one thing for too long or boredom would set in, using up one block and then moving on to the next whether you were finished with the first or not. Enough had trouble applying this system. If the truth was known, Motorboat had a bit of trouble himself. Enough found it would not work for school hours. They were beyond his control. But with anything under his control, he followed Motorboat's system. Control was a big thing with Motorboat.

Enough decided on a half hour for eating. The remaining thirty minutes he would look for blowdown.

Fate decided otherwise.

At the end of the meadow, where the path entered the hardwood stand, his feet pursuing a life of their own while his eyes gazed skyward, Enough stumbled over the body of a man. He very nearly fell on top of old Mr. Fremont, done in neatly by a blow to the rear of his head—right at the edge of the hardwood stand and under the direct gaze of Robbie, who still snoozed, back against a rock, up on the ledges of Indian Mountain.

Robbie, lord of all he surveyed.

CHAPTER TWO

Enough felt the apple pie rising to the surface. He took a deep breath, turned on his heels, and sprinted back down the path to the lodge. He banged on the kitchen door and a frowning A.E. confronted him.

"What in the world is the matter? Didn't I tell you not to bang on that door? What's wrong with you, Enough Peabody?"

"It's not me. It's Mr. Fremont. He's in the hardwood stand."

"The hardwood stand? What's he doing?"

"He isn't doing, A.E. He's done. Done-in, I mean. Dead." Enough struggled to get the words out.

A.E., who had come back down from the tower room to recheck her grocery list, carefully placed her pencil on the long table. "Are you sure? Did you touch him?"

"I'm positive. I know dead when I see it." Enough shivered. "There's blood on his head. His face is kind of sideways so I knew him right away, but he's pretty messy."

A.E. strode out of the kitchen, turning down the long hallway until she reached the wall phone outside the bathroom door. She dialed instinctively. The lodge kept numbers for the fire station, the hospital, and the sheriff's office pinned on the wall alongside the oak phone. She reported the death promptly, gave the lodge's address, and returned to the kitchen, where Enough was telling his story to a skeptical Peggy.

"Let's go." A.E. took Enough's arm and they moved quickly down the path, across the meadow, and towards the woods.

"He's dead, all right." Looking down, Enough felt the pie churning about in his lower regions. "I got to get out of here. I don't feel so good." He turned toward the lodge, but the pie won, and for a few minutes Enough forgot the body at his feet.

A.E. stood resolutely, nerve ends at attention. "He must have hit his head. But how could he have, it's the back of his head that is all blood. The only rock is the big one in the middle of the meadow. There's just woods trail here. Could someone have attacked him?"

Enough wiped his face and decided he felt better. His mind was racing to recall all the crime stories he'd read.

"I don't think it was an accident. I think somebody hit him on the back of his head. How could he walk with his head all open like that? I think he was murdered."

A.E. shivered. The sun, almost noon high now, seemed to be fading behind clouds that were moving into the steel blue August sky. The air felt cooler, a chance breeze riffled the hardwood stand, the tops of the maples, beeches and oaks stirred gently, and the meadow grass rippled softly. The meadow, usually so warm and inviting, was suddenly a foreign land, and the hardwood stand, a haven for small animals and birds, suddenly seemed dangerous and threatening.

The woman and the boy turned in unison and walked quickly back toward the lodge—not knowing that above them, on the mountainside, Robbie still slept. And off to his right, hidden behind a tall pine, a figure watched through binoculars.

"Too close. Too close. "It was almost a whisper. "That boy may have to go."

Dick Eggleston was already tired at noontime when the call came in to the sheriff's office. Dick had been up nearly all night with Frieda, who was definitely having trouble carrying their first child and who needed someone to talk to in the midst of her weird dreams. Frieda was sure the child was starcrossed. Even Dr. Easton was beginning to have doubts that Frieda could carry to term. Dick sighed and wondered whether it had been sensible to have a family. Maybe Dr. Anna Easton had been right. Maybe they shouldn't have taken a chance after Frieda was forty. Maybe it would all end in disaster. It was a race to see which was more important, Frieda or his job.

Today the job was winning.

Moving his cruiser with speed and precision down Route 26, Dick perused the thought that only a quirk of fate made Frieda his wife. It might have been A.E. Gibbons. The three of them had grown up together, gone to the same school, ridden the same school bus, and played on the girls and boys basketball teams. Now, more than twenty years later, A.E. would stop by to bring Frieda apples every year from the lodge's old Blue Permain tree, and Frieda in turn gave A.E. a jar of home made mincemeat every Thanksgiving. Both women knew their places might have been exchanged, but this was territory neither explored. Their friendship had endured through the years.

A.E., tall and stringbeany in her old tweed skirts or jeans, her long red hair beginning to show gray; A.E., with her spindly legs in boots making one think of Vita Sackville West.

And Frieda, little, cuddly, blonde Frieda, who had giggled in the corners with boys while A.E. stalked by them; Frieda, who was still small but not quite so blonde now and certainly a lot less cuddly. Frieda looked like the wife who attested to the value of a cleanser on a T.V. commercial. Next year she might do a testimonial for diapers.

Dick regeared his mind to the call at hand and, turning off Route 26, drove into Bryant Pond and out over Rowe Hill Road, looking for the long, narrow, dirt ribbon that led into Indian Lodge. After nearly half a mile, a driveway appeared off to the left, and Dick turned, noting the gravel base looked untended with small islands of grass shooting up through the stones. Dick remembered that A.E. had hired Enough Peabody to be yard boy for the summer.

Evidently, there was more work than Enough could handle.

The porch floor was freshly painted, the log columns supporting the porch roof appeared to have been restained, but the barn looked seedy and the roof shingles on the lodge were beginning to curl.

A.E. was trying, but it seemed to be a losing battle.

Dick brought the cruiser to a halt in a shower of dirt and gravel and got out to meet Enough, who had jumped halfway down the lodge's steps.

"Boy, I'm glad you got here. Looks like we got a real problem on our hands." Enough was excited. Murder didn't happen every day in his life. He was storing up real news to tell Motorboat tonight.

"Where's A.E.?" Dick moved straight ahead to the screened kitchen door.

"Here." The tall redhead offered a cup of black tea to the trooper. "I thought you might need this."

"What happened?"

"Enough found Mr. Fremont dead in the hardwood stand. I walked back, and we looked again. I wanted to be sure he was really dead. Sometimes he" — she pointed to the boy sitting on the edge of the old Windsor porch bench— "Sometimes he exaggerates."

"I never. Not this time. No sir, he's real dead, Mr. Eggleston. I know dead when I see it. I know dead."

"O.K. Who is he, A.E.?"

"Mr. Alexander Fremont. He comes to the lodge every summer. He's retired from a ministry in Virginia, and he's always been interested in the history of Maine Indians. He goes up to the ledges and the caves on the mountain every day."

"And—" Dick led her gently.

"Well, I pack him a lunch, and he walks up and spends most of the day up there, poking about. He must be about seventy-three by now, but he doesn't look it. I mean, he didn't." A.E. looked distraught. "He left this morning around eight. He didn't actually say he was going to the caves, but he always goes there."

"Did he always go alone ?"

"No, sometimes Bill Bannerman went up with him. You know Bill, he lives over on the back swamp road past Robbie's shack, and Bill's sort of a hermit. He comes in the summer to that old camp of his. More like a hovel, I'd call it. But he knows a lot about Indian history in this area. I think he wrote a pamphlet about Indians once. Anyway, Mr. Fremont and Bill spend a lot of time together. Did"—

"All right. Let's go look. That sounds like the ambulance now." Dick made a note on his pad. He shoved it in his pocket and started across the lawn, with Enough and A.E. behind him. Through the snake fence, through the meadow, past the beehives, and toward the hardwood stand, the three marched in single file. Suddenly, Dick turned.

"Was he going to meet Bill today?"

"I don't know. Bill usually comes the first week of June and stays through September. Mr. Fremont hadn't mentioned seeing him."

Minutes later the small group stood looking down at the medical examiner, Dr. Anna Easton, who did double duty as an Oxford County general practitioner and substitute examiner. She knelt over the body for some time, then motioned Dick to one side.

"Well, he didn't do this to himself. Looks to me like it's pretty simple. Someone took a good swing at him and connected right on the back of his skull. There's a lot of blood loss. That's all I can tell at the moment."

"Would he have died immediately?" Dick bent down to note the rather surprised look on Mr. Fremont's face.

"Pretty nearly. He couldn't have lasted long with that blow. Wasn't too long ago, either. Within two or three hours, I'd say. He should have known someone was behind him." Dr. Anna frowned.

"He was absent minded," A.E. volunteered. "He was like that at times. Lost in thought. I could put the tea tray right down by him, and he would hardly know I was there until I spoke."

"In any case," Dr. Anna continued, "that blow finished him. He must have just dropped down. Such a senseless thing. It's getting to be a senseless world."

Dick turned to A.E. who was finding it hard to control her shaking hands. "Did he carry a lot of money?"

"Never. He was a thrifty man, and if he went anywhere, he only took a few dollars. He never took anything up to the caves except his lunch, his water bottle, and his notebook. I don't think he had any enemies. He retired from the ministry a few years ago—someplace in Virginia. I think he was a Methodist. In quite a small town. How could this have happened?" A.E. was incredulous.

Dr. Anna shook her head. "It's not like it used to be. People just seem to up and kill each other—drugs or liquor or money. Some jailbird might have been walking along the path and been mad at the world. People beat each other up all the time. We used to live in a little savannah of safety here in the county— no longer."

A.E. shivered. "I don't know who to notify. I think he did mention a niece once, but I don't know where she lives."

"There may be an address or phone number in his papers. I need to go through his room, A.E. I'll need the key." Dick rose from his hunkered-down position and shoved his notebook in his pocket. The medics placed the body on a stretcher and Dick marked the ground below.

"I'll need to cordon off this territory while we search for a weapon." He turned to the two deputies who had just arrived.

"I'm going back up to the lodge with A.E. to look at that room. Key?"

A.E. shook her head. "We don't have keys to the rooms, we never did. A couple of years ago I did price door locks but the cost was so high I gave up the idea. Most of the guests are the same ones each year anyway. They kind of liked the idea of not having to lock their doors. There are hooks inside to hook them when you are inside the rooms, but no actual keys. When we have a new guest they're always amazed, but we've never had an incident."

"Until now." Dick snorted.

Enough had been standing by listening to every exchange. "Can I come up with you? Maybe I can help. Boy, a real murder." His voice was excited.

"Well, he certainly didn't do it himself." Dick sounded exasperated. "I have to look at the room alone, Enough. A.E. will show it to me. But you can walk through the meadow and the hardwood stand with the deputies. I'm looking for the weapon. Keep an eye out for anything."

"Right." Enough was excited. Wait until he saw Motorboat tonight. There would be more than the usual dinner conversation.

"And, Enough, one other thing." Dick looked thoughtful. "If you do find anything, don't pick it up. Call one of the deputies."

A.E., standing by Dr. Anna, was puzzled. "Dick, why was he here, anyway? He wouldn't have been back here this time of day—unless something happened up there and he had to come back to the house."

"Or," said Dr. Anna, who still hated the face of death even after all the years it had been her partner, "unless someone was after him."

Upstairs in the minister's room, a corner one with windows facing two directions, Dick searched methodically while A.E. stood watching, feeling as though they had no right to invade the old man's privacy. She felt her hands shake again, something that had happened more than once lately, and something she hated to admit. There was no putting it off any longer, she would make an appointment with Dr. Anna.

"He used that little desk often, Dick. I used to bring his tea up to him in the late afternoon after he got back from the caves. If there is an address book, maybe there'll be a phone number for his niece. I feel I should call someone, but I don't know who." A.E. stood in the doorway watching Dick sort through a small pile of papers.

"Here it is." He held up a small green book, worn and with part of its back missing. "It's full of names. Do you have any idea what hers is?"

"Nancy—Nancy something and she lived in Delaware, I think. I know he said she was the last of his family, and he only saw her at Christmas. Wait a minute, her husband teaches at some university in Delaware—maybe the University of Delaware?"

"This sounds like it." Dick handed the book to A.E. and motioned her out of the room. "Go make a call. You're shaking, A.E. Look, why don't you just sit down a minute. Who's helping you here at the lodge this evening?"

"No one. I have to shop this afternoon, and then it was just going to be dinner for Mr. Fremont and the honeymooners. They'll be back later—they went off on a walking trip for the day. We have new guests coming in tomorrow. Peggy helps me every morning and evening now. It's going to be a busy week. But tonight was only Mr.Fremont and the Shermans."

"The Shermans?" Dick was rapidly covering the room, looking under the bed, in the closet, going through the rest of the papers on top of the little painted chest of drawers that matched the painted rustic bed. He hadn't missed an inch of the room, but he knew he also hadn't gained an inch of information unless the address book held a clue. Maybe the niece would know something when and if she arrived to take care of the body.

"Mr. and Mrs. Charles Sherman. They like to be called Chuck and Debby. They're from Boston, and I don't believe they notice much, they are so full of each other." A.E. smiled. "They came on Tuesday. Mr. Fremont came on Wednesday, so they only saw each other at the evening meal. They didn't talk much. I don't know where they went today. I packed them a lunch, and they were gone by nine o'clock. They read about us in the paper, of course. Mr. Wortham's column."

Dick grinned. "I heard about that. You're going to be busy this summer, A.E. Not much time for fishing."

"And you know what I say to that. Damn." The tall woman turned and headed along the Turkey Red carpet covering the scuffed wooden hall floor. If she had to be invaded by the outside world, maybe she'd even have a cordless phone.

Wonder how far out from shore it would extend? I might even be able to take it out fishing.

Halfway down the stairs her mind came back to the day's activities. Peggy should vacuum this carpet, it was beginning to look grungy. Rooms needed to be made up for the weekend. Murder or not, she still had to shop for food this afternoon or tomorrow morning early, and it was vital to make an appointment to see Walter Desmond at the bank. She could not put off asking for a loan any longer. The three old bathrooms were just that, old bathrooms with chipped linoleum and fixtures that weren't always reliable, walls that needed painting, and windows that needed new curtains. For all the charm of the old lodge, things did not work well, not well at all. The old heating system gurgled and choked and hammered and banged, and the steam radiators generated a cacophonous tune every time the furnace was lit in the fall.

We have charm coming out of our ears. But I'd like to be able to flush a toilet and be sure it won't overflow. I'd like to able to take a bath, and not run out of hot water. And, heaven help me, I'd like to just be alone and not swamped with all these tourists. Next time any one gets mired down in the mud I'm going to leave him there.

Money. No matter how you looked at it, money was needed to repair the lodge. So, Walter Desmond, here I come.

A.E. suddenly laughed. *For a woman who wants to be a Hermit I am certainly in the wrong business.*

The phone in Delaware answered. It was the right Nancy. She was surprised at a call from Maine and shocked to hear of her uncle's death. She listened closely while Dick, who came immediately to take over the conversation, explained Mr. Fremont's death. Nancy would come on Monday, not before, and would stay a few days. No, she couldn't think of anyone who would want to hurt him, he was respected by his congregation, and no one would think of harming him. Perhaps it was an accident?

Dick talked for a few more minutes, ending with assurances the body would be taken care of until she arrived to make plans. As he turned away from the phone, Peggy quietly appeared with a tray, almost as if she knew that sustenance was needed. Dick smiled when he saw the piece of apple pie, remembering A.E.'s description of Enough's reaction to the body. He accepted a cup of strong tea from Peggy.

His eyes followed the girl as she left the room.

He turned toward A.E. "Now, the meadow and the foot of the hardwood stand are off limits. The room, too, for a while. I may have to search again. But you can go ahead with your weekend plans for booking. When Nancy comes on Monday, she can go into her uncle's room if I'm finished with the examination. I want to talk with these Shermans. What time do you think they'll be back? And I want to see if I can locate Old Bill if he's in the area. You, A.E., you go see a doctor and get a checkup. You're too white and your hands are shaking again." Dick was solicitous.

"It's just strain, Dick. Business problems and being invaded by all these people and not having time to fish. And now this. You always did tell me what to do. How's Frieda? Does she feel any better?" A.E. recognized the strain between the couple. Frieda had tried to speak of it in one of their conversations but abruptly changed the subject herself as though she did not want to face what was happening to her marriage. The two women had been awkward with each other, both knowing they might say more than they wished to, both feeling trapped and misunderstood, Frieda with her pregnancy she could not come to terms with, A.E. in her self-imposed solitude.

Perhaps Frieda is stronger even though it appears the other wat around. I haven't half the energy I need, and I've never lacked it before. I mustn't let anyone know that-except Dr. Anna.

Dick finished his tea and rose to leave. "Frieda's still having trouble. Dr.

Anna's making her spend part of each day in bed. If we can get through this next month, she ought to be O.K. She's real short-tempered, but I guess I'd be, too, if I felt as miserable as she does. I don't know, A.E., if we should ever have thought of a baby at our age."

Dick shook his head and looked down at his scuffed cowboy boots, the one imperfect part of his impeccable uniform. "Well, enough of that. Thanks for the tea. I'll be back this evening to talk with the Shermans after their dinner, so ask them to stay here when they come back, please. And, A.E., make an appointment with Dr. Anna, will you? Who'm I going fishing with if you get sick?" Dick grinned, gave her topknot a tug, and departed.

A.E. patted her hair thoughtfully. Actually, she had never gone fishing with Dick. The word in town was that he sometimes strayed. Remembering his glance at Peggy, she wondered if he had ever fished in that direction.

CHAPTER THREE

Dr. Anna Easton drove slowly along the River Road, her thoughts on the dead man at Indian Lodge. Almost fifty years of medicine stood behind her, but Dr. Anna still hated death. At first, right out of Johns Hopkins and new to country medicine, she thought she would outgrow the feeling but that had not happened. Today the old stomach sickness had risen like clockwork, the same as it always did when she first looked upon a body that had met violent death. After the first look things settled down, but that first look always made her want to drink her daily scotch immediately rather than waiting until the agreed upon time of six o'clock.

For Dr. Anna, who enjoyed her liquor, had made a pact with herself that it would be one scotch daily, and that one after six o'clock. Like all the other pacts she had made with the fragility of her soul, she'd kept it, but none of her patients knew of the struggle she had gone through to toughen herself against the world.

Dr. Anna could keep secrets. She knew the value of the unspoken word.

Something was bothering her about Mr. Fremont. The look on his face? That was it, the look. It was as if he was seeing something—no, listening to something. The eyes looked and listened. Could eyes listen? Was that possible? Yes, it was, it was as if they were almost squinting, as if he had been straining with his eyes as well as his ears—listening?

"It's a pity." Dr. Anna mused aloud. "It's just a damn pity. He probably never did anything but good in his whole life and some weirdo had to come along and kill him." She began to think of what she had known of Alexander Fremont.

Alexander, retired from a ministry he had secretly found boring, had sought out the services of Dr. Anna only once—last summer, when he had taken his usual three weeks in August at Indian Lodge. A splinter in his ring finger had festered and Anna had taken out the jagged piece of wood, drained off the pus, and ended up going out to dinner at Mariah's with her patient. Nothing too important came of all this except a few scotches enjoyed on rainy summer afternoons when Alexander was supposedly taking his late nap at the lodge before tea and Dr. Anna was supposedly awaiting late patients in her office adjoining her old red Cape on the River Road in Bethel. Things never progressed much further, Alexander's three weeks were up, and he'd promised to call her when he returned to the lodge this summer. Well, he'd been there since Wednesday, and today was Friday. Whatever might have developed was over now. Dr. Anna sighed. He had been an exceptionally nice man. There were too few around.

Alexander had looked forward to the three weeks in August. He had known the Gibbons family since Susan, A.E.'s mother, had decided to keep the lodge open after her husband's death. Then she had been killed in a car accident, and A.E., at age twenty-five, returned from Europe to run the lodge herself. Alexander came every summer, and he had watched A.E. grow from a rather worldly young woman into a retiring spinster. A solitary woman who wanted only to spend hours in her canoe fishing for trout in the pond.

The Indian history of the area had fascinated the minister. The faint trail leading around the lakeshore and the path leading upward from the hardwood stand onto the mountain had become almost closed in with brush. Every year Alexander had found he had to clear out more undergrowth. At the top of the mountain ran two long ledges, one directly above the other and both below the series of interlocking caves that bored into the mountainside. The ledges and the area in front of the caves were natural lookouts for anyone scanning the expanse of the long, narrow valley and its boomerang-shaped pond. The Abenakis had frequented this area every spring on their run down from Canada and upper Maine, and here they had sometimes met with Indians from the area around Lewiston-Auburn, Indians that came up the Little Androscoggin in their canoes, portaging around Snow Falls and like areas, until they turned left to arrive at Indian Pond. There the tribes gathered, Wabanakis, People of the Land of the Dawn, and there, high above the pond, in the caves, the shamans may have met to ask for guidance for their people in the coming year. The lake on one side of the valley offered fresh fish, and the meadows along the shore offered small game and an ideal spot to make camp. How much they used the caves was not mentioned in the scant history of the region, but some arrowheads had been found there and once part of what might have been a cooking pot and a ragged piece of what might have been a wide splint-basket. Certainly that could not have been too old; some authorities on northeastern Indian baskets claim that wood splint plaiting came into New England by way of some Swedish people who in turn taught it to the Indians around the beginning of the eighteenth century. At the most, this scrap, if it was authentic, could have been no more than 250 years old. Little remained of the oldest baskets—the damp, wet, winter weather of New England is not conducive to preserving baskets as is the dry climate of the southwest. No Anasazi baskets here.

Alexander, resigned to the effects of the climate, looked for arrowheads, bones, and possibly a burial spot. Certainly the caves were natural havens for life moving through this mountain valley.

He spent almost every day in the caves during his summers at Indian Lodge. He measured, he dug, and he took pictures when the light allowed. He kept notes carefully in his small black notebook. The caves had not yet been designated as a National Historic spot by the state. They were almost forgotten except for a few locals and the Boy Scout troop. Still, Alexander would never have disturbed any treasure, had he found any, without some authority, although who he would have gotten it from, he didn't know. It was A.E.'s property, and the trail winding downward on the far side of the ledges crossed Robbie's land and led onto the dirt road that went to the three cottages on the north side of the lake. There was an old granite monument with a stone cache surrounded by a sagging iron fence at the far side of the swamp, but this and a few Indian history books written about the area were the only signs that this valley once was a gathering place for the separate families on their way to and from the coast.

Only Alexander and old Bill Bannerman cared enough to search for further evidence of past life in the valley.

Old Bill Bannerman fit no known pattern. Even A.E. knew nothing of his history. Where Bill came from or what he had done for a living was a mystery. In early June, usually when the black flies were at their peak, he opened his camp back off the swamp road in behind Robbie's shack, a one-room cabin with outbuildings built of vertical cedar posts arranged in soldier like precision around an inner shell of two-by-fours and wide pine boards. An old granite stone fireplace gave him enough heat for the summer and he cooked on an ancient 1920s oil stove, the kind that carried its oven on top and smelled so bad he had to air out the camp every now and then, more now than then. An old tin sink in one corner held a hand pump bringing water out of a cistern beneath the floor. Bill lived simply, read voraciously, hiked with the aid of a staff, and spent long hours researching and writing about the area's Indians. It was natural for the two older men to meet and spend their summers exploring the mountain and the caves.

This Friday morning had been no different. Alexander had hoped to find Bill at the caves. The minister had arrived on Wednesday, but it had been Friday before he'd assembled his gear and been ready for the mountain. Bill had no phone. The men communicated through letters in the winter, made their plans for the summer, and trusted to luck (in Alexander's case, God) that they would eventually both show up at the same time on the mountain. Alexander had written Bill over the winter telling him of a new place he had planned to dig. Bill had answered he would join him at the end of the first week. He would bring a small bottle of "oh be joyful" to celebrate their digging, and they would share it at lunch. Today might be the day, and all the way up the trail Alexander, puffing more than usual, thought of the weeks ahead. He plodded up the path, noting places that needed cutting back, and finally reached the caves. He placed the lunch and water bottle carefully in a small cranny he had used each year, laid the black notebook and pencil on another rock within the cave, and scanned the area at the rear corner where he had left off working last August. The pile of rocks seemed the same, perhaps a little different. His eyes narrowed and he wondered who had been in the cave. He knew where he had stopped last summer. He knew this cave with his eyes closed he had spent so much time in it.

The pile of rocks definitely seemed to have a different arrangement.

Alexander squatted on the dirt floor and gave this some thought. Who else even cared about the caves?

Carefully he removed several small rocks from an area he had last worked. He had been sure last summer that there could be an opening in this area, an opening that might expand into another space behind the wall. His hands flicked dirt, and the opening reappeared, just as he had remembered. He reached in, almost up to his elbow, and felt the opening widen, and said aloud, "Perhaps another room. What—"

His hand touched a cold object, round, certainly not stone, certainly not native to the cave. For a moment he thought of the "feelie boxes" his Sunday school children had made one year, lined with whatever their imagination dictated, made for the Christmas bazaar. People reached in and guessed the contents and won a prize if they could guess all of the objects.

No church bazaar here. His hand pulled the object forth and he stared at a large coffee can, three-pound size, with its plastic cover still in place. He hesitated for a moment, then pried off the lid. The morning light was best at the cave entrance, so he moved forward to inspect his find. Whatever was in the can was wrapped in plastic. Carefully he unwound the wrapping and stared at the neat rolls of bills. And he knew, without question, that this was not meant to be found.

Alexander was a gentle man. But he was not a foolish man. Very quietly he pushed his notebook and pencil into his pants pocket, left his sandwich and water bottle where he had placed them and, holding the can gingerly, the lid back in place, he started back down the mountainside. As he did he saw Robbie, who had just settled in on the ledge below. He knew there was no help there. He set off at a brisk pace and had just reached the edge of the hardwood stand when he knew there was someone behind him. His eyes narrowed, he started to turn, and he felt the terrible pain.

He died without ever knowing what he had found. What it meant, or how it would affect the lives of so many in this valley.

CHAPTER FOUR

Dr. Anna, driving with her mind on the past and Alexander, suddenly realized she had reached the red Cape. She maneuvered her old Ford station wagon into the garage that attached itself to the cape by a glass-windowed ell and stepped out with a sigh. Only three o'clock, not yet time for the longed-for scotch, but it was getting closer. There were a few patients due in by appointment, and her answering service told her Mr. Jackman was expected at four-thirty and Mrs. Evans needed a prescription renewed at the Bethel Pharmacy. She slumped into the brown leather chair behind her desk and stared into space, still thinking of Alexander Fremont.

The phone rang, and she picked it up with her right hand while her left removed her sturdy British walking shoes. She scratched her feet in turn and elevated them to the top of the worn walnut desk.

"Dr. Easton here." She hoped this would not be a long conversation. She felt decidedly old.

"It's A.E., Dr. Anna. I guess I really ought to have a checkup. I don't feel like myself."

The older woman sat at attention. "I thought you looked a little peaked. Figured it was Mr. Fremont's death. What's the problem?" The age old question.

"I feel shaky sometimes. It's probably low blood sugar or some such thing. Maybe I need iron or extra vitamins. Dick asked me why I was shaking. When people begin to notice I guess I'd better see you. Could I come in next week?"

One eye on the appointment book's blank spaces, Dr. Anna searched for the closest. "How about Tuesday at two o'clock? If that suits you."

"I'll be there." The sigh of relief was barely audible.

It was nearly three-fifteen. The deputies still searched the hardwood stand. A.E., standing in the middle of the big kitchen, looked at the wooden counter running down the middle, its marble top resplendent with a fresh pound cake and two apple pies, one minus two slices. There were chicken breasts marinating in herb sauce safe in the recesses of the square refrigerator, and vegetables were washed and neatly stacked in an old basket, one of Robbie's, that took up the bottom shelf of the cooler. The ice cubes were ready, good decaf Copenhagen coffee sat in the old tin canister by the stove pot, and the preparations for tonight's meal appeared to be finished.

A.E., shaken by the morning's events, would have liked a nap, but shopping in Bethel had already been delayed by hours and she still had to go to the bank. She would make two quick phone calls and then drive into town.

Lee Heaward answered the phone at High Meadows. When she heard the rather British voice, Lee's mind backtracked to the valley at the foot of Indian Mountain. Five years ago Lee had sold a cottage to Walter Desmond, the president of one of the area's banks. Walter had said he needed a place "to rest my mind." Lee and Meg Bundy, owners of Carriage Trade Realty in Paris, had just that year listed a cottage on Indian Pond. The Pennsylvania owners had found it too far to drive up in the summer, and it was exactly what Walter and his wife Carol wanted. A place to relax, and grow vegetables. A place to sit in the sun, to fish, and have a respite from the banking world. Everyone was satisfied, and Lee, driving into this small, almost unknown valley, had turned down the wrong road in the beginning, just as Mr. Wortham had, and found herself charmed with Indian Lodge and its owner. Since then A.E. and Lee had become firm friends, not seeing each other for long spells of time, but each time picking up their conversation at almost the point they had left off. Friends of the heart, one might say, last forever.

This afternoon, A.E.'s conversation with Lee was brief.

The lodge owner wanted the realtor to look at the lodge from a professional view and give her some advice on financing. A.E. told Lee briefly of the death, the police investigation, and asked her if she might be able to stop by the next day, Saturday. Lee would try to find time. They left it at that, knowing there would be more time for details later.

The second call was to Walter Desmond. Yes, the bank was open until five today, and he would be happy to see A.E. He'd just heard of a death at the lodge. What could he do to help?

So A.E., her heart wishing she might be pulling weeds in the bed by the snake fence with the yellow roses spilling over, drove to Bethel and made swift work, even on a Friday in August, of buying groceries for the weekend. At almost a quarter to five she walked into Indian Mountain Bank to face Walter Desmond and finally ask for a new mortgage.

Walter Desmond sat behind an English mahogany desk that filled nearly one side of his office. The desk's surface, mirror finished, was barren except for a set of pictures displayed under beveled glass. Walter's wife, Carol, his prize saddlebred mare, Datura, and his two English setters, Casco and Key, were in the spot of honor. To one side was a picture of a large Hubbard squash that had taken first prize at the Fryeburg fair. On the other side, in perfect balance, was a double picture of his camp on Indian Pond, the left side showing it in the original shape at purchase and the right side showing it spruced up in its present condition. Walter had begun to acquire possessions early on in his banking career, and he was not above letting A.E. feel, on this late August afternoon, that she might have shared some of this bounty had she paid more attention to him in their school years.

For Walter, also, had grown up with Dick and Frieda and A.E., and he had seen prospects in this tall gangly girl with the laced up boots and the topknot of red hair. This girl who would rather fish than look to her future, ride horses yelling like a banshee, or swim the length of the pond before the ice was hardly out in the spring. Then, with A.E. off to Europe and out of sight of the local young men, Dick had married Frieda and Walter had fallen in love, expeditiously, with Carol, whose father came to Maine summers and who introduced Walter to the banking world. A.E. was gone forever, it seemed, a rare bird not to be caged but only admired.

Walter had never spoken these thoughts. That would have been outside his character. But it was evident as he casually mentioned the exploits of Casco and Key at their last Massachusetts field trial. A.E., who had recently lost her last dog, an old border collie who did little more than sleep on the porch and mix with an occasional skunk, A.E. knew exactly what Walter was getting at: she had missed her chance. She sighed and hoped they would get over this fence quickly so she might get on with the reason she was sitting on the other side of the magnificent desk. It was late and she found her hands beginning to shake again. *Money.*

Money and time had driven her, this August afternoon, to listen to Walter reliving their past. She needed to stop his talk of field trials and start on her problem. She needed time to breathe and pay bills and do some renovation at the lodge. What she really needed was time to go fishing. And here he was, talking about setters.

Suddenly, Walter Desmond remembered he was a banker.

"What I don't understand, A.E., is why you don't sell the place. You'd have a considerable amount to invest, and you could buy something smaller or save a piece on the pond and build a cottage. You wouldn't have to work; you keep saying you hate having to have guests. You could just putter around the garden and raise those old-fashioned roses you like so much and maybe even buy that little Morgan mare you've always wanted. Why do you even want to fix that big place up? Remember our high school days?"

A.E. remembered. Walter knew he'd hit a tender spot. A.E. had been a good horsewoman. The Gibbons family kept horses up until the year Susan Fox, A.E.'s mother, who had married John Gibbons, was killed in a car accident in

1963. A.E. had come back from Europe to take over the lodge. Bills she hadn't dreamed of existed, and, in her early twenties, A.E. was thrown into the unknown world of business. Her father, John Gibbons, a bomber pilot, had died ferrying planes over the Mediterranean in World War II, and Susan, a rather sporty lady, was left to run the big lodge on the pond. Susan had kept horses, run the lodge haphazardly, and sent her daughter off to study in Europe after two years in an American college. Susan had no idea of business and the lodge began to slide backward. Once self-sufficient, it started to add to the morass of debt Susan accumulated. So when A.E., still in her twenties, inherited, she faced a good reputation with repeat customers, but also a pile of bills along with beginning complaints of faulty sinks, no wood for the fireplace and no hot water. With a diminishing bank balance, A.E. began to face reality.

She had struggled valiantly. The horses were the first casualty. The sports cars turned into one small Jeep, and A.E.'s own wardrobe of tweeds and Irish sweaters, although fashionable, became a staple. She cooked and waited table herself, hired a cleaning girl to help only in the spring and fall, and painted, papered, and carpentered as best she could. Finally, as the years slid by, she realized she could not maintain both inside and outside. Enough had arrived two years ago when Motorboat, fishing the lake for the first time, saw the red-haired woman paddling an old birchbark canoe and bailing water at the same time. She was using worms, and Motorboat watched her cautiously as she hauled in a good-sized brook trout. So Enough came to be yard boy and Peggy came to be kitchen help, and things were a bit easier. Mortgage payments were made on time, but the lodge was awash with deferred maintenance, and now that Mr. Wortham had recommended it, something had to be done.

Money. The things people have to do.

"I don't want to sell, Walter. The lodge has been in the family for four generations. John Fox, my great grandfather, built it in 1875. I want to keep going if I can. Look, I've brought some figures for you." She handed him a torn notebook page, ragged edge foremost, covering the glass-topped desk at exactly the place where Casco and Key pointed, frozen in time.

"The Morgan mare," she said, "will have to wait."

Walter sighed and shook his head as he looked at her offering. "Look, you have to fill out a regular financial form. This won't do. You need a financial statement and a projection. We'll have to get an appraisal on the property—"

"I called Lee Heaward. She's coming by tomorrow. She'll give me some idea of the lodge's worth," A.E. interrupted.

"Well, that's fine, but we'll need a full appraisal. That is, if we do give you the loan. Let's start with these papers. It shouldn't take more than six to eight weeks if the loan's approved. But you have to bring these forms back to me first." Walter felt a little out of charge of the situation— somehow or other the conversation did not seem to be going in the right direction. "Think about it. Life would be much easier for you if you sold."

"And what would I do, Walter? Where would I go? And have my own pond to fish in? I do admit I'd like a horse again. But I have lots of exercise. Just going up and down those stairs is better than a treadmill. No, I don't want to be anyplace else. You know, Walter, someone said, 'How do you know unless you go?' And, Walter, I've been."

The banker, a bit miffed by all this philosophy, rose in dismissal. "Leave the papers with my secretary when you bring them back. By the way, what happened out at the lodge this morning? I know you had a death."

A.E. gave a brief explanation. Walter nodded. "I know all those trails up the mountain. I walk up there sometimes or jog along the road that goes by the camp. Well, I don't imagine it will hurt your business too much."

A.E. looked surprised. "I never really thought of that. I just thought of Mr. Fremont and that I'll miss him. His niece comes on Monday. I have several bookings for next week. There's another couple here right now. It is upsetting, but I don't know what else to do. Dick is handling everything. I have to go, Walter. Thanks for listening to me."

Walter, who a moment ago had wanted to end the conversation, suddenly felt the need to prolong it. "Who's at the lodge now?"

"Peggy Canevari helps in the kitchen, and Enough Peabody has been doing yard work this summer."

"I've heard of that boy. He's the one lives with Motorboat, doesn't he? How did he ever get that name?"

"He's a seventh child. His mother had a hard labor and the first word she said after the birth was "Enough." I guess Mr. Peabody, who was a bit inebriated, thought she wanted to name him that. So it went on his birth certificate. Nobody checked until much later. Then they left it. I kind of like that name, it fits him." A.E. chuckled.

The atmosphere in the office lightened. The banker reached out and touched the woman's hand. "It seems a long time ago we were in high school, doesn't it? Dick and Frieda and you and me. We certainly all scattered in different directions. I'd like to stop by and see you next week, maybe talk about old times. Renew our friendship, so to speak. What do you say?"

"Delighted." A.E. gritted her teeth. "Bring Carol with you. I haven't seen her in ages." She retrieved her hand and walked rapidly to the door.

Walter's eyes narrowed, his hands twisted the notebook paper. He turned away as A.E. left. Then he picked up his phone and buzzed his secretary.

"Bring me some coffee, will you? Black. Make it hot for a change, and hurry up. I don't care if it is five o'clock."

CHAPTER FIVE

While all these events had been taking place— Mr. Fremont's body removed from the hardwood stand, the comings and goings of the state trooper and the sheriff's department, Dick's short exploratory walk up the trail— Robbie still slumbered, snug in his spot above the valley and Indian Pond. His body, slumped to one side, was settled far back in against the granite rocks. Anyone looking directly down at him, as Alexander Fremont had, would notice the still form, but anyone else, from any other vantage point, might think him no more than another rock on the ledge below the caves. That is, unless they happened to be using binoculars. Then they might have known it was Robbie.

The afternoon wore on, Dick left to find Old Bill, Peggy continued her work in the lodge, and Enough finished his outside work and headed home to Motorboat, carrying the news of the day with him. A.E., at three-fifteen, went to Bethel to grocery shop and see Walter Desmond at Indian Mountain Bank. And Robbie still slept.

The basketmaker had walked a long way that morning. Although he knew every mountain trail, he was wearier than usual. Robbie was a frugal man, living mostly on vegetables he canned himself, on the wild berries of the valley, and gleanings from neighbors' orchards and gardens. Actually, he depended on his own ingenuity. Occasionally he shot small game, although he hated to kill any living creature. A.E. gave him honey when she extracted her hives yearly and helped her place hay around them for the winter. Walter Desmond sometimes allowed him to gather the last of the garden vegetables at the end of the summer. And he had a small income from the sale of his baskets. Old Bill brought him a small bottle of whiskey yearly and Robbie stored it away (for medicinal purposes only) as his mother had told him. Sometimes, when the wind blew about the small camp and the temperature inside was nearly freezing, Robbie made a comforting drink of whiskey and hot water and honey. Alone now, removed from most human intercourse, Robbie lived with the spirit of his mother by his side, guiding his hands as he wove the sturdy ash baskets. The genes of his family had never supported life much beyond fifty years and Robbie was close to that number.

He slept a long while. He woke with an aching body from his slumped position, and an aching head due to no food since his bowl of oatmeal and mug of coffee in the morning. He pulled on the pack basket with a grunt, took the applewood staff, and started down the mountain, this time to the path leading toward the three cottages and his own camp near Old Bill's. Suddenly he remembered he'd started out that morning to talk with A.E. and he turned in his tracks, readjusted the basket, and retraced his steps over the ledges, down the mountain trail, and into the hardwood stand. Within ten minutes he emerged directly into the meadow where two deputies were unrolling tape to add to the already cordoned off area.

Robbie hesitated. He was puzzled. He did not trust people in general, and these two men in uniforms unrolling yellow tape across his path seemed alien to his world. He turned to retreat to the woods. One of the deputies, looking up from the widening path of yellow ribbon, gave a yell.

"Hey you, over here. Where did you come from?"

Robbie hesitated—usually he turned away when someone spoke to him, unless they were buying baskets—but this seemed a different situation. "I just been up on the mountain for a spell."

"Doing what?" The man sounded decidedly cross.

"Oh, look, Jim, I know him." The second man spoke. "He's Robbie Moulton, the basketmaker. Did you see anyone up there, Robbie?"

"Just trees." Robbie drew back.

"Don't be funny with me." Jim was irritated. "Someone was killed near here. Maybe you ought to come along with us to see Dick." He turned to the second deputy. "I think Dick ought to see him." He placed his hand on Robbie's shoulder.

"Let's go back up to the house. I'll phone in from the car." He motioned towards the lodge and gave Robbie a slight push.

"No. I was only going to see A.E. I didn't do nothing." Robbie's voice had a whining sound not unlike a cat pushed too far by a dog.

"Just come along now." The second deputy was kinder. The man looked harmless, he really seemed too slow to have committed murder, and he was evidently just an area local wandering in the woods. However, nothing should be overlooked and Dick could make the decisions. Maybe he even should be searched.

With a reluctant Robbie in tow, the two men walked across the meadow toward the lodge. Robbie argued no longer. He knew once they arrived A.E. would sort things out, and so he resigned himself to putting up with these figures of authority, which was what they seemed to be, until they found A.E. Then, he was sure, it would be sorted out and he could go home. He was puzzled as to why they thought he might be involved in whatever they were searching for, but he knew he had nothing to do with whatever it was. He decided he would leave it all up to A.E. Besides, Robbie had a policy, taught to him by his mother, of ignoring things he didn't understand.

Just pretend you don't know. Stay out of the way. They'll leave you alone.

He would not think about this. It would go away. And if it didn't, A.E. would make it go away.

Reaching the cruiser, the deputy named Jim phoned headquarters for Dick Eggleston. The second deputy, the one more disposed to Robbie's plight, sat the basketmaker down gently on the lodge's porch.

"Just stay right here. We are going to need to talk with you further."

Robbie shook his head. "I didn't do nothin," he repeated. The people of the swamp had spent generations staying out of trouble. One thing they had been taught as soon as they could walk was to stay out of the way of the law. Swampers, they had been called, and Robbie was the last one.

His heritage came to the fore. He felt trapped. He was the ferret, gone to ground.

"I didn't do nothin." It was a whine.

The first deputy returned. "Dick's over at Bill Bannerman's. He'll be here directly. Maybe we ought to see what you got in the pack, Robbie?"

What Robbie had in the pack, among other things, was a short-handled wooden mallet with dried blood on its face. Used quite recently.

"This damn road ought to be condemned." An hour previous to the discovery of the bloodied mallet in Robbie's pack basket, Dick Eggleston was bouncing his cruiser over outrageous ruts and sinkholes on the road to Bill's cabin.

Dick's head rose twice to meet the roof of the cruiser, his stomach was standing by, but only under duress, and he wanted nothing more than to turn back and get out of what was rapidly becoming a single-file Indian trail.

"My God, how does he ever drive in here?" Dick gasped as his head again hit the roof.

Old Bill, rocking gently on the open front porch, smoking his pipe and drinking Jack Daniels neat, heard the commotion and patiently waited. Generally they gave up and didn't bother him. Once in a while a persistent one made the trip in and then Bill just pretended he was deaf. This one sounded different, cantankerous like. Determined you might say.

He sighed and took another pull on his drink. A man of my age, he thought, needs his comforts. His eyes narrowed as the police cruiser negotiated the last turn in the trail and came to a shuddering stop. Like a horse ridden too often and too far, it seemed to give a last twitch, and the motor died. Dick caught his breath and stepped out.

"If I have any tires left I'm lucky. No wonder you're a hermit. Nobody can get into this damn place."

"That's the idea." The corners of Bill's mouth twitched. "I'm surprised you made it. Must be something real important for you to come all this way."

"You don't know, then." Dick hesitated.

"Tell me, then I will." Bill sat forward.

"Alexander Fremont's been killed. Enough Peabody found him this morning right in the edge of the woods off the meadow at Indian Lodge. A.E. said he'd gone off earlier up to the caves and might meet you there. So—"

The front legs of Bill's tipped-back chair met the floor with a thud. The old man leaned forward to look at the young trooper. His eyes were cold ice blue.

"Alexander? That man never hurt a soul. Who did it?"

"We don't know. That's why I'm here, we only know he was hit hard on the back of his head with a blunt instrument. He died quickly. Did you see him this morning?"

Bill shook his head. "No, I was late getting up, and I didn't start out until around ten o'clock. We'd been writing back and forth all winter, but we didn't have a definite day. I usually didn't dig without Alexander, although I walked up there a few times in July this year. Just to sit on the ledges. This morning I felt kind of tired, and I went up halfway and then sat on a rock by the trail for a while, turned around, and came home. My head's been feeling fuzzy lately. Thought I'd try it again tomorrow."

"Are you sure of the time? Did you see anyone?" Dick's voice was sharp.

"It was nearly ten o'clock. I didn't see anyone. I had a headache, and I gave it up for the day."

"A little too much drinking, Bill." Dick snorted. He settled himself into the second porch chair and eyed the old man. "You're sure you didn't see or hear anything?" The trooper made notes on his pad and made himself comfortable in the straight chair. Bill didn't seem too hospitable.

"Told you I didn't."

"Well, I'm guessing someone knew his habits if they killed him on the mountain. He was coming back down the trail and we can't figure out why. A.E. says he should have been in the cave. Somebody knew his routine."

"Meaning me?" Bill shot the question.

"Possibly. It could have been an accidental happening, he might have come upon something he shouldn't have. And then someone had to shut him up. Or it could have been planned. You dug with him. What sort of things were you finding?"

"Odds and ends. Arrowheads. A part of what looked like a cooking pot. Alexander thought there might be more passageways and crevices back in the cave. Did he have his notebook with him? He might have written something down."

"It was in his pocket. Along with his pencil. But A.E. says there was his lunch and a water bottle."

"Yup, I remember that pencil stub. He was a thrifty man. He'd write down measurements and anything he thought important every day when we'd have our lunch. I kidded him but he was always hoping to find something relating to the Red Paint People. Alexander was a born optimist."

"But you never did?" Dick was listening intently.

"No. Like I told you. Arrowheads. A piece of bone that might have been human. Mostly animal bones like squirrel or rabbit. Those were recent. There were mountain lions here once, they could have brought prey into the caves. We weren't very scientific. No carbon dating. But Alexander said these were the sort of cave formations that the Indians might have used during their trek up or down from the coast. They would pitch camp by the lake. Their tradition was that higher ground was scared and the shamans might have gone up to the caves to seek help from their gods. Certainly the caves could have been used for storage, the southwest Indians did that along the Canyonlands trails. Maybe there might have been a burial cache."

"So he might have come on something." Dick was following Bill's words.

"It's possible. He'd written me a letter saying he thought he'd found something on his last dig. I left early last year. Before he did. And we were planning to have a celebration with a little Jack on our first time together. We never had a set time plan. We just knew we'd find each other eventually. I'm here most of the summer, although I was away part of July, but he's only here for three weeks. We knew we'd find each other sometime during his first week." Bill paused. "I'd like to help you find who killed him. There aren't too many people like Alexander."

"How about yourself, Bill? You're kind of an enigma to the townfolks. Past history? We're going to be asking everyone that question."

"Thought you might come on to that. Past history. Well, I was a schoolteacher in South Dakota early on. Then I spent twenty years in jail. Served my time. Came out and took up teaching again. Taught at a school for special students in the southwest. Some of them Indians. I still teach a bit, I go to Tucson every winter. And come up to Maine for the summers. You know the rest."

"Twenty years in jail?" Dick stared at the weatherbeaten face, the still thick gray hair and the ice blue eyes. Here was a man with the apparent strength of Mt. Rushmore.

"Twenty years in jail, Bill?"

Bill lumbered to his feet and disappeared into the camp, reappearing with a jelly glass in his hand. Carefully, he poured a small amount of Jack Daniels into it and offered the glass in Dick's direction. He refilled his own and reseated himself in the straight-back chair. He leaned back and drew carefully on his own glass. Then he looked directly at the trooper.

"Guess it had to come out sometime. Murder, Dick. I did twenty years in jail for murder."

CHAPTER SIX

Bill's hands were steady as he held them in front of him for a moment, as though in testing them he was testing himself and his ability to relive old memories.

"No sense dwelling on the past. I hit a man in a fight and he died. I didn't intend it to happen; we were young bucks fooling around, and I hit him hard in the wrong spot. It was a long twenty years, Dick. There's nothing more to say."

"I'll have to check it out, Bill. You know that. South Dakota, you said?"

"A town called Estwing. An Indian name. That's one reason I liked helping Alexander. Twenty years is a long time, and I did a lot of reading in jail. I studied the Plains Indians, learned about the Blackfeet, about the pictures Curtis took of different Indian tribes. You know, he even actually took pictures of North West Coastal Indians in their war canoes. Actual moving pictures. Then I began reading about the Red Paint People and the eastern tribes. The Algonquins and the Abenakis. There wasn't much written then, not like now. But I acquired a solid background. When I came out here I met Alexander, and we both wanted to know more about that cave. We both had a feeling it was a sacred place. Maybe where the shaman went to speak with the spirits. It seemed as though we were just beginning to find the secret. Poor Alexander. I'll miss him."

"Did he know your past, Bill?"

"That's what was the best of all. One day I asked him if he minded I had been in jail. He just studied on it for about five minutes. I didn't know if he was ever going to answer. Then he leaned over and patted my hand and said 'The Lord doesn't mind, so why should I?' We never mentioned it again."

Dick rose, placing the emptied jelly glass on the old wooden table. "I'll talk more with you later. I have to go back to the lodge to speak to the Shermans this evening and then check on Frieda. Just don't plan to do any traveling, Bill. I want to keep track of you."

"I'll be here through the summer as planned. I'm going back up to the caves after a while, not right away. Don't know's I can face it right away. Are they off limits?"

Dick shook his head with hat still anchored in place.

"There's no reason they should be. The meadow and the area just into the woods where his body was found are off limits, but other than that you can go anywhere. We've closed off his room at the lodge but his niece comes Monday and after she's looked through his things, I'll open it again. If you find anything, Bill, let me know."

"What are we looking for? Exactly."

"I don't know. We haven't even found the weapon yet."

Time is both enemy and ally. At the very instant Dick spoke these words to Old Bill, Robbie's pack basket was being searched. Probing fingers found the short-handled mallet coated with dried blood, and Robbie, still befuddled and unbelieving of this new development, was a prime murder suspect.

Dick took leave of Bill, refusing another jelly glass. "I'm out of here. It's almost six now, and I have to check on my wife. That is if I can get back down your damn cowpath."

Halfway through the woods the word came in from Jim and Arnie at the lodge that they were holding Robbie Moulton. And Dick knew that dinner with Frieda would once again be late.

A.E.'s old four-wheel-drive Jeep turned in the road leading down to the lodge just as Dick's cruiser pulled off Rowe Hill Road. He followed her; a stone flew back on his windshield and he wished A.E. wouldn't try to ask more out of her old Jeep than it cared to give.

How the devil it even passes inspection I don't know, he thought as he followed close on the rust-stained vehicle.

The second cruiser was parked in the circle and even though it was only six o'clock on this August evening, the lodge showed lights in the kitchen and in the big porch lanterns. Gathering clouds predicted heavy weather ahead. Dick helped A.E. with the grocery bags, placing them on the long kitchen table. He walked quickly into the small office room off the kitchen where Jim and Arnie confronted an increasingly terrified Robbie.

"What's the story here?" Dick looked at the two deputies.

"We found the mallet in his backpack. He'd been up by the caves, he says, then came down through the woods and we picked him up just at the edge of the hardwood stand while we were taping. He says he went to sleep up on the ledges. Didn't see anything and must have slept for a long while. He says he didn't know the mallet was in his backpack. At least that's his story."

"But this is Robbie. What's going on here?" A.E. entered the room. She had seen the police cars and thought them only a continuation of this morning's problem, but now, here was Robbie looking terrified. Her protective instincts surfaced and like a mother cat defending her kitten, she prepared to do battle.

"This is Robbie. My friend. He has every right to be up at the caves. He brings me baskets, takes care of the bees, and has always been on the land. He wouldn't hurt a fly."

"A.E., they've found a mallet with dried blood on it in his pack basket." Dick's voice was low and troubled. He too knew a little of Robbie's history, and he knew things did not fit. Somehow, he had to sort out these developments.

"Look, A.E., go make a pot of coffee will you? I haven't had anything to eat since breakfast nor have the boys. Robbie, try to remember what happened. Exactly. What were you doing in the woods anyway?"

Dick knew the answer when he asked the question. But he knew Robbie, and he knew if the basketmaker could talk a bit about something he understood he might regain enough composure to be helpful. Dick could smell the fear within Robbie's small body. If he refused to talk they would make slow progress.

A.E. shifted from foot to foot. She watched Robbie's face with dismay, realizing that Dick was asking for help.

"Look, I'll make a plate of sandwiches and I've some pie." She left the room to return to the kitchen, where a troubled Peggy was gathering silver for the dining room tables.

"A.E., I don't believe Robbie did anything bad. Not Robbie."

Peggy's small round face shone with a glow that was beginning to turn heads among the men in town. Her hair was finespun blonde gathered in curls at her neck and with a wisp hanging down on each side of her ears. She wore almost no makeup, but the small nose and the blue eyes gave her a gamin appearance, that instead of being short and well formed, she was tall, almost as tall as A.E. and only what can be described as skinny. The face shouldn't have gone with the body. The face, pure elf, sat on a model's body. But over Peggy hung an aura that would beguile more than one man in her lifetime. She was now sixteen. No wonder Enough was under her spell. He little realized the maturity of his heart's desire.

A.E. suspected but had never gone beyond speculation. Peggy did a fine job in the kitchen and in the dining room, whisked rooms clean in short order, and what she did on her off time was her own business. Once in while there was a call for her in a masculine voice, but that was rare. Peggy kept business in one pocket and pleasure in another.

Tonight A.E. blessed the girl as she fitted slices of bread into sandwiches and poured out the cups of steaming coffee. In a matter of a few minutes Dick and the deputies were regrouping and Robbie was pecking at a roast beef sandwich and a glass of milk. A.E. sliced pie and handed around forks and plates, gathering up residue. For a moment no one spoke.

Then Dick tightened his belt and started again-this time listening first to the deputies describing Robbie's emergence from the woods, and then Robbie's almost unbelievable tale of sleeping for several hours, during which time the mallet, he thought, now that he gave it some thought, must have been removed from his pack basket and then replaced after it had been used as a weapon.

"Not hardly likely." Jim, the first deputy, snorted.

"But it could have happened." A.E. had been listening closely.

Dick bowed his head. He didn't like what he had to do. It wasn't going to make him a very popular man in the county.

"I think I ought to take him in for more questioning, A.E. I probably won't have to hold him. But I have to consider all factors. If something more turns up and I feel I have to put him in jail, I'm sure he could get bail. But I can't just walk away from facts."

"Robbie hasn't any money." A.E. felt frantic.

"Well, I haven't any choice." Dick felt smothered, angry that he was going to be cast in the role of the unfriendly law, knowing what would happen as soon as the newspapers had the story. He knew there would be reporters back at the county seat, and he disliked reporters. Things could get twisted. He was disliking this case more and more, but there did not seem to be a choice. He had to dig deeper. Or, at least, appear to dig deeper.

"We've read him his rights, A.E., but you may want to get him a lawyer. He may need bail. I'm not sure yet—"

"Don't tell me, I know. Go with Dick, Robbie. I'll take care of things. I'll get help. Just go with him and don't make trouble."

Confusion showed on the face of the small, stooped man. His hands twisted and picked at his old corduroy trousers. His eyes darted from side to side. Like a ferret he was hopelessly trapped in a world he knew little of and tried hard to avoid. Somehow this world was falling in on him.

"I didn't do nothin" he whispered.

A.E. almost in tears, saw the men out with their prisoner. She left Peggy to wait on the Shermans who had just entered the dining room, and hurried to the hall to use the phone.

On a small screened porch overlooking the orchards that rode like ships across the greensward, a man and a woman sat in the twilight enjoying their evening coffee and each other's company. Unlike in many respects, yet alike in their great love of the land, Lee Heaward and Hod Cole were a relatively comfortable alliance. Both had experienced difficult times in their lives, but both were old enough to realize they, like ships, had come to rest in a quiet harbor.

"With no questions asked." Hod had said.

"And none answered." Lee had replied.

Tonight neither of them wanted to answer the insistently ringing phone. Hod had spent most of the day working in the old tack room in Lee's barn, now in the process of being renovated into an office room for his maps and timber charts and pictures and books on the history of logging in New England. These had all been part of the bookcase area in his Sumner cabin, but slowly, as he and Lee began to consider putting their lives together, they had agreed that he would move in with her at least for a year's trial and he needed to have space for his own business "doin's" as he put it. Right next to the horse stalls was an old tack room, unused for several years. Lee had planned for some time to ream it out and renovate it, but it was a natural place for Hod's accumulation. With an old pine table, a few office chairs (Lee insisted they have cushions), and some pine sheathing to dress up two of the walls, electric heat put in for chilly days and a phone, new windows out the side, it had developed into a space that Hod was beginning to enjoy. Not only was it his space, but the timbermen who frequently needed to talk to him could feel comfortable here just as could the little old ladies who sought Hod to selectively cut their family woodlots. Lee said no more after the initial offer of the tack room but sat back and watched Hod become more involved than he had been in many years. She knew instinctively that she must be patient if this relationship was to work.

"Are you going to answer that?"

"I'm forced to. I forgot to turn on the answering service. I guess I'd better answer in case it is Meg."

Lee rose, but within two minutes she was back on the porch. "Hod, we should go right away. That was A.E. Gibbons calling from Indian Lodge on the pond. One of the guests was murdered this morning, and Robbie Moulton's been taken in to be questioned. There's a possibility he may be the murderer."

"Robbie!" Hod was on his feet. "Robbie Moulton wouldn't hurt a fly."

"That's what A.E. said and we know that. But he'll need bail if they decide to hold him and he is very confused. A.E. was almost in tears. She's generally self-contained. She said she'd meet us at the jail."

"I'll get Bill Todd. He'll arrange bail if it's necessary." By now Hod had the phone in one hand while he buttoned his sweater with the other.

"It could rain tonight, Lee. Bring some gear, will you?"

Lee was moving swiftly, putting the last of the dinner in the refrigerator, stacking plates in the sink. Kate, who sensed the unusual haste, cocked her gold-and-black head to one side.

"You're staying home, old girl. Take care of things." Lee patted the Gordon setter's head. Collecting rain gear, she picked up her shoulder bag and joined Hod, who was already looking to see if his Jeep had sufficient gas. Wrapped in their own thoughts, they were silent most of the way to the jail. Hod, generally taciturn, had made it clear to Todd that if Robbie was held, he wanted to get him out on bail as quickly as possible. He hated to think of the basketmaker penned up for even one night.

It took a while. Robbie's questioning took time, but A.E.'s almost hysterical concern, Lee's reassurances, Hod's cold, clear analysis of the situation, and finally, Bill Todd's own expertise helped in his release. Dick has gotten as much information as he could from the small, ferret-like man, and there was no reason to hold him further at that time.

Within two hours Robbie was released, and they stood by the two cars deciding where he should go that night.

"Robbie, what do you have back at your place for animals?" Lee's concern for all living creatures was evident.

"Batch of chickens, they mostly scratch for themselves. Two cats. And Howard."

"Howard?" Hod raised an eyebrow.

"My swamp pony. Have to get his water pail filled every day. But he mostly eats grass. I ought to see to Howard."

"I didn't know you had a pony." A.E. showed surprise.

"He was out in the swamp. His foot was caught in one of them old fences. I cut him loose. Wasn't anybody's pony, far as I could see. But he's real smart, he held just as still when I helped him. Had him a couple of weeks now."

"Have you heard of anyone losing a pony?" Hod turned to Lee, who knew most every horse owner in the county.

She shook her head. "I've never heard of one lost. But if Robbie says he was caught in a fence, he was. Maybe you'd better go back to your home, Robbie. We'll drive you. And, A.E.—"

"I'll come over in the morning, Robbie, and bring you some food." A.E.'s hands were shaking again.

"Don't have to. I'll walk to the lodge. I got to tell the bees."

"What?" A.E. looked puzzled.

"Tell the bees. They got to know someone died."

"What are you talking about?"

Hod interrupted. "It's an old custom. Dates way back to early Europe, I think. When there is a death you go tell the beehives. Otherwise bad luck comes to the house where the death occurred. The bees have to know. I haven't heard anyone say that in years."

Robbie nodded his head in agreement.

"Thanks, all of you. I won't run away. And I'll be there in the morning, A.E. I got to tell the bees."

CHAPTER SEVEN

By now it was ten o'clock at night. Robbie had been deposited back at his cabin and his three saviors had looked at Howard. With weariness A.E. drove her old jeep down the driveway to Indian Lodge, and Lee and Hod headed back down Route 26 for High Meadows. Both cars had joined in taking Robbie home, admittedly because the two women's love of horses made them anxious to see this animal who had been found caught in a swamp fence. Burrs still matted his reddish brown coat, but he lifted his feet at command and gently chewed on a carrot Lee found in her jacket pocket. Lee promised grain and A.E. proper hay. Puzzled, the three left.

Now, Hod drove carefully along the main road. In deep thought, he brushed his forehead once or twice with a lean brown hand.

"Lee, I don't get it. The whole picture. Something's out of whack. Robbie sitting up there on that ledge asleep most of the day, someone's coming along and using his mallet to murder old Mr. Fremont, who seems to have been going in the wrong direction. And then that someone putting it right back in the pack basket for it to be found. Seems to me somebody's awful smartass to just take that kind of chance. And what's the point in murdering that old man? What did he do or what did he know that was so threatening to someone they'd kill him?"

"Maybe he saw something. Something that wasn't supposed to be seen. Or maybe he found something. You know, I remember A.E. talking about him last year, how he'd been coming to the lodge for years. I never talked with him myself. But I have to go out to the lodge again tomorrow. I promised I'd try to give her an idea of a market value of the property. I can't do a regular appraisal, but I'm going to recommend she have one done. I can give her some idea of a range of what it might be worth."

"What time are you going? I just might see if I can scout up Dick Eggleston and talk a bit with him. Then I'm going to check on Robbie. We're sort of responsible for him staying around here."

"I don't think he'd ever run away. First of all, where would he go, except further back in the woods. He's lived in the swamp all his life. That's all he knows. The swamp and how to make those beautiful gathering baskets."

"Lee, you know more people. Where did you find him?"

Lee smiled and put one hand on the back of Hod's neck to begin a gentle massage. "In my travels. I guess I know every back road up and down this valley. Meg and I have listed a lot of country property. When I sold that camp on the other side of Indian Pond to Walter Desmond, I saw Robbie's sign on a tree. A handwritten sign on a piece of old wooden shingle. BASKITS. I had to stop and look. And there they were, three of them laid out on a board across a couple of sawhorses. I got to talking with Robbie, and I've known him ever since."

"Did he ever think of trying to sell them in the real world?" Hod turned the car into the driveway of High Meadows.

"The swamp is Robbie's real world." Lee sorted her legs out and swung herself out of the Jeep. "Hod, where do you suppose that pony came from? People just don't lose ponies and horses without looking for them. That puzzles me."

"Me, too. There should have been something in the paper if he'd strayed from a farm. They'll go a long way. I knew one once walked all the way over Hebron Mountain. It started on Route 117 and just walked Singepole Mountain and down onto Hebron Back Station Road. But then he was an ornery pony. Howard, if that's what Robbie wants to call him, seems like a pussycat. I don't know how old he is, but he seems pretty mellow."

"I think he's still fairly young—I looked at his teeth when A.E. was checking his feet. Outside of the fact he's all matted with burrs, he's in fair shape. A.E.'s going to call the vet in South Paris to see if anyone's reported a pony lost. Hod, I'm tired. Bedtime for me."

Hod opened the kitchen door, scooped up Kate, who was dancing joyfully in anticipation of a walk, and ushered Lee inside.

"Look, you go on up. Kate and I'll check out the horses and have a short ramble. Blowing up a storm from the feel of it."

An hour later the storm hit. Rain lashed High Meadows Farm. Robbie's camp and Indian Lodge were taking the full brunt of the storm up through the valley, and somewhere, secure in a bed in a warm house, a murderer again thought over the day's events and wondered if there had been any mistakes. It had been a spur-of-the-moment decision, triggered by events not anticipated. But it had been accomplished. Chances are it would be an unsolved case and life would continue in its pleasant pattern.

Except for the fact that nosy boy might have to be exterminated.

Chapter Eight

Five o'clock Saturday morning.

The storm had been short and fierce. Puddles of water still lay on the low spots of Indian Lodge's lawn, and the garden along the old snake fence showed shredded effects of the whipping winds. A patch of purple asters had been flattened, and the yellow roses, which had been at the end of their bloom, were now quite done. There is a sadness to a flower bed after a storm. You know it will revive, but there is sadness at the abrupt loss of beauty.

A.E. sat on the steps of the lodge, gazing at the pond. The sun had risen over the far mountain, and the warmth of its rays, even at five on this morning, touched the surface of the lake and caused the mists to rise. The only sounds were the early morning birds, the coo coo of the mourning doves in the trees along the shore, and the splash now and then of a fish rising far out in the pond. A.E. sat, legs akimbo, cradling her cup of coffee, and her thoughts turned back to the day before. So much had happened in such a short space of time—incredible to believe Mr. Fremont dead and lying on a gurney while the medical examiner explored his old body, incredible to believe that Robbie could have found a pony caught in a fence in the swamp, and incredible to believe that Robbie could be suspected of murder. The sun climbed higher, and A.E. still sat lost in her thoughts. He would be here soon, he had promised to tell the bees. A.E. knew Robbie. He would come, and it would be soon.

Bees are out only with the sun. Robbie, walking doggedly along the trails toward the lodge, knew he was a little late. In another few minutes he would pass the turnoff and come out on the lake side of the lodge, facing the gardens and the beehives. He would be in time, but only just. And thinking about it, as he had with his slow mind as he trotted along, he had been wondering what he would say. He knew his mother had told bees—she had spoken of this among all the other things she had spoken of during the winter hours they had spent in the cabin alone. But she had not told him exactly the words she had used, whether she sang to them as she often did to Robbie when she was showing him how to make baskets, or whether she just thought it and they knew from her thoughts what she was thinking. Robbie knew how that worked too. Sometimes he found he could tell what was going on in other people's minds, and then he had to be careful and not let on he knew what they were thinking. That was the most important thing, not to let on. Only certain people could you trust, could you tell your thoughts.

A.E. was one. Lee Heaward was another. Look how they'd understood about Howard the moment they'd seen him.

They had only asked a few questions and Robbie had been proud that he'd thought of the idea he'd found Howard caught in a fence. He didn't really believe it was a lie. They had certainly come over an old fence when they were returning from where Robbie had really found him. If he told them exactly what happened, they might take Howard away. And he didn't want that to happen. Howard had told him. Howard had spoken to him and let him know right at the beginning that matters were out of control and that he wanted to go with Robbie. And Robbie knew exactly what his thoughts were. He had always been able to read animals' minds since he was a child.

Robbie knew exactly what was in Howard's mind. He rescued him without question. But under what circumstances he did not want to even tell A.E. or Lee. Only he and Howard knew the secret.

Possibly Mr. Fremont may have known something. Maybe that was why he had been killed. It was too much for Robbie to put together. Maybe that friend of Lee Heaward's might help. Hod Cole, that was his name.

He was now at the lower edge of the lodge's lawn. The hives were just ahead and he could see a few bees beginning to emerge. He was just in time. He stood quietly in front of the three hives, unprotected except for his own thoughts, and spoke in a low singsong voice.

"There's been a death, friends. An old man. They say I might've done it, but I wouldn't. Robbie wouldn't hurt anyone. Now you know, friends. There's been a death."

A.E. strode across the lawn as Robbie turned away from the hives.

"Come in and have some breakfast, Robbie. You can't have had much sleep. I heard you speak with the bees."

"I told them, A.E."

"I know, Robbie." Gently she reached out and touched his shoulder.

No one was up in the lodge. The Shermans were still asleep and Peggy would not be in until eight. Enough arrived around eight-thirty. There were three couples and one single booked for tonight, and all of them would probably be in by four o'clock and ready to sit down for six-thirty dinner. A.E.'s Saturday night dinners followed the same pattern the lodge had laid down for the past thirty years. Mr. Wortham had written of these Saturday night dinners, and newcomers to the lodge always asked to be booked in for the feasts. Tonight there would be lobsters and corn on the cob and three different types of salads, hot biscuits with rosemary, and three desserts. Along with plenty of hot coffee and the famous lodge punch.

But this morning there was Robbie, and A.E. laid bacon strips in a pan, took eggs from the old refrigerator, and cut thick slices of homemade wheat bread to place on the grill.

"Here's your coffee." She handed him a thick white hotel mug with a green lined rim, and indicated the sugar and honey. "Help yourself. How's Howard?"

"He be fine. He's a good pony, A.E."

"He certainly is." A.E. was puzzled. "What have you fed him for the past two weeks, Robbie? I'm kind of surprised you didn't come over and tell me about him. He ought to have a little more than that meadow grass."

"Grass was all I had, A.E. Maybe if you go into town you'd get me something for a pony. Maybe I can get some hay from Danner's farm. Maybe I could make something to fit Howard's back to carry two bales home."

A.E. placed the heaping plate in front of Robbie, added a knife and fork, poured herself more coffee, and sat down beside him.

"Robbie, I have an old rig out in the barn. It's just a cart for one horse—it must have been made for milk cans. High wheels and the back slides out. But if we could rig up some kind of a harness I'll bet you could train Howard to pull it."

"He's trained already." Robbie savored the bacon and added jam to the thick slices of toast.

"How do you know?"

"Well, I just know." Robbie realized he might have said too much.

A.E. was puzzled. "Look, Robbie, if there's something else you should tell me. You're sort of out under our care right now. They probably really can't hold you for murder, even if they wanted to. But anything you know you should tell. Or is it that you're reading Howard's mind?"

Robbie nodded. "That's it. I can tell what he knows. What he thinks." He looked keenly at the woman sitting beside him. "You can too, can't you? Sometimes."

A.E. nodded. "Sometimes. And I don't know how. It isn't something I talk about with many people."

"Me neither. I'm slow but I don't be crazy." He stood up and pushed the plate away. "I thankee. You're a fine lady, A.E. Best next to Mumma. Could I see the cart?"

The cart occupied a corner of the old barn. Traces of blue paint still remained. The shafts were strong and still held the rings for the driving reins. The body of the cart had once held milk cans. The floor was still strong enough to hold a few hay bales and Robbie could reinforce it with a couple of pieces of wood. A.E. took down old harness and between the two of them they rigged a passable driving gear within a half hour.

"Now, all's we need's Howard." Robbie was smiling. A.E. agreed. "I'll be busy here all day. We have people coming in this afternoon. And the state trooper will be back soon. Why don't you go get Howard and bring him up here and then you can drive him back? No, wait a minute, I think Motorboat's home this weekend. Maybe he can haul it over for you. Let me call him, Robbie."

They walked out of the barn to meet Dick Eggleston, who was just coming in the driveway. A.E. hurried to make tea while Robbie stood in the early morning sunlight now spreading over the lawns and gardens and the edge of the lodge nearest the lake.

Dick, looking at this small brown man, knew in his heart that Robbie had not killed Mr. Fremont. But the law has to go through the formalities.

"Robbie, you know you shouldn't leave this area. You are still a suspect."

"I know. I got to take care of Howard, anyways. Me and A.E. been fixing a cart up. And I told the bees."

Dick was a modern sheriff trained out of state, with knowledge of computers, drug tests, every new way to catch criminals. But he also knew enough not to cross country customs. Who knows what might happen if the bees hadn't been told ? He shook his head but patted Robbie on the shoulder. "Just stick around."

"Dick, I'll be serving breakfast before long. And I haven't had mine yet, just coffee. Eat with me, and Peggy will be here to do the Shermans so you can interview them. Enough will be in soon. I have to call Motorboat before I forget it." A.E. was persuasive.

Dick nodded and went back to the cruiser to phone in while A.E. called Motorboat Jones, who at that moment was sitting down to breakfast with Enough.

"O.K., Enough, now start from the beginning." Motorboat adjusted his stomach over his belt buckle that pronounced TRUCKER. He poured cereal into a bowl already thick with blueberries. "Just start from the beginning and don't get carried away."

Enough made short work of the previous day's events and ended with the fact of Robbie's being taken away by the police.

"I was in bed before you came in last night. I thought I could stay awake to tell you, but you came in awfully late."

"Truck broke down on 495. I got to work on that most of this weekend. But there's about as much chance of Robbie Moulton killing anyone as me marrying Princess Di. Where's Robbie now?"

"When I left, A.E. had called Hod Cole and Lee Heaward and they were all going to meet at the jail. Peggy said—"

"Ah, yes, Peggy. I wondered when you were getting to that one."

"Peggy said they'd help Robbie. That's what A.E. was talking about on the phone. Something about they all knew him and knew he wouldn't do it. A.E. called Mr. Fremont's niece earlier. She's coming Monday. And I got to get up there a little early this morning 'cause there's three parties at least coming in today. And Peggy—"

"You still chasing her?"

"Not really chasing. She's fun, though. Tell you the truth, I think she's got someone. But she's awful close-mouthed."

"I bet she is. Look, I'll—" The phone rang.

While Enough finished his cereal, Motorboat listened

quietly. Sparse with his answers, he replaced the phone in its cradle and finished the sentence he'd begun.

"Like I said, I'll take you up to the lodge. That was A.E. I'll take the small truck, there's a cart we need to take over to Robbie's swamp cabin. Seems the law didn't hold him. Enough, just how much poking about in those woods did you do when you helped the deputies look for a weapon?"

"I was there for about an hour. I didn't find anything. I didn't go up to the ledges. That's where Robbie was asleep, at least he said he was."

Motorboat, taking the keys off the hook in the kitchen, looked at the boy. "I got a feeling you better keep an eye out all the time. Something doesn't feel quite right, Robbie asleep and all that going on down below. If what you say happened and someone really did take a mallet out of his pack, kill Mr. Fremont, and then put the mallet back, there was an awful lot going on up there. Robbie's asleep, Mr. Fremont's climbing around, someone—the murderer—is up there, and who knows who else. Just be a little careful. None of this makes a lot of sense."

Which were exactly the same words he used half an hour later as he helped A.E. pull the cart out of the barn while Dick talked with Robbie.

"I know that, Motorboat, don't you think I've thought of it?" A.E. was exasperated. "This whole thing is almost more than I can fathom. It started out to be such a quiet year, but that writer got trapped on the road in mud season, the next thing I knew we were written up in the out-of-state papers, and now I've got all sorts of bookings. I even had to go see Walter Desmond and redo my mortgage to give me some money to fix up the bathrooms and the bedrooms. And Mr. Fremont was killed and now I seem to have more bookings than ever. I don't know where all this is going to end, and I'm not sure I want to do this much business. And I liked Mr. Fremont. He was family, and there isn't much family left." A.E.'s voice trembled.

"You're not even going to have time to go fishing." Motorboat was teasing.

"Don't say that. This morning early when I had my coffee on the steps and I looked at the mists rising, I wanted to be out on the lake, but there were things to get ready in the kitchen. Then Robbie came, and the whole day seems to be rushing by. Motorboat, my life is all wrong now. It's not what I want at all."

"Well, I told you how to fix it. If you'd quit trying to run this lodge, just close it up, and—"

"Are you going to start that conversation again?"

"No ma'am. I'm just picking it up from where we left off. If you don't want to talk, O.K. But how about making a date to go fishing tomorrow morning? It's Sunday, I'm not back on the road until Tuesday. I'll get here about five and we'll take the canoe out for two hours, until seven. Just fish off that right bank. I'll bring some worms. We'll just be quiet like. You bring out some coffee. I promise I won't plague you."

A.E., her long fingers twined on the edge of the faded blue cart, had to smile. Motorboat never gave up. Since the year when they had met in their respective boats (hers a birchbark canoe) on the pond, when their lines had tangled and tempers had flared (mostly hers) Motorboat had been smitten with this tall, gangly, bad-tempered, stubborn woman. Motorboat, whose head was balding, whose shirt was forever parting from his pants, who was probably five years younger than A.E. but looked five years older, Motorboat was smitten. He who lived and talked eight-wheelers and stock cars and who drove monthly from Maine to California was a victim of unrequited love. What they had in common was fishing, she with worms and he with lures. From their first meeting he was out to catch Amelia Earheart Gibbons.

Persistence won. A.E. agreed. With one last tug of the rope they maneuvered the blue cart up the ramp onto the trailer. Motorboat lashed it down, and as A.E. turned toward the lodge, Lee and Hod arrived.

Hod, who like Lee knew everyone in Oxford County, shook hands with Motorboat and admired the trailer's baggage.

"Don't know but what that's an antique. I haven't seen one of those carts in years. Where you going with it, Motorboat?"

Motorboat explained about Robbie, Howard, the hay hauling, and the fact that A.E. had the cart in her old barn. Hod and Motorboat both shook their heads as they discussed Robbie, both agreeing on his character being opposed to murder and both feeling something was not, as Hod put it, "according to whack" in Mr. Fremont's death.

Inside, Peggy, who had just arrived, started the coffee urn and mixed a batch of muffins. A.E. showed Lee the downstairs great room and the dining room of the lodge and the upstairs bedrooms and baths with the exception of the room Mr. Fremont had stayed in and the one in which the Shermans still slept. The two women ended at the tower room and stood looking out on the pond and the mountain.

"You can see right up to the ledges. I never realized that." Lee admired the view.

"Yes, as far as the curve in the lake, then the rest is hidden. But if I used binoculars I could look right up to the path that goes up to the caves and the ledges. I suppose someone could look down here," A.E. mused. "If you can see them, they can see you. Isn't that the way it's supposed to be in mystery stories?"

Lee nodded. "That's the theory. When I'm at an auction and I look in a mirror and see someone I know they can also see me. Funny feeling. You mean you think someone could have been watching the lodge. And Mr. Fremont?"

"I don't know what I mean. It's just a feeling." A.E. shook her head. "Let's go down. I'll bring out some coffee and muffins, and we can all talk on the porch. Peggy will let me know when the Shermans are ready for breakfast. She can handle them alone, anyway. As soon as they have eaten, Dick wants to talk with them. He didn't have a chance last night."

The two women walked down the stairs, along the old faded Turkey Red carpeting, Lee's hand sliding along the golden oak woodwork, the carved mouldings of the doors and windows. On the second floor a window seat overlooked the lawns and the pond, and down on the main floor the old bookcases along the center hall were carved with acorns and flower symbols.

"Someone gave time and thought to this place." Lee admired the woodwork in the main great room.

"Great-grandfather Fox. It's been in the family for years, Lee. I don't want to lose it. So I guess I should be grateful I can run it as a lodge. I just like my privacy."

"I understand." Lee touched the younger woman's shoulder. "I've fought within myself for years to know whether I want to sell real estate or not. I hate some of the things that have happened in New England. But now I've come to reconcile myself and live with it—I just build my own world within. That may not be the proper way to deal with it, but it gets me by as they say. You may have to do the same thing, A.E. The lodge has to be the real world for you—the pond your private world. And Motorboat?"

"You noticed?"

"It would be hard not to. Hod thinks highly of him."

"Well, he's a good fisherman." A.E. laughed. "Wouldn't we be the most unlikely couple?"

Lee smiled. "I would wager some say that about my own arrangement. Don't worry about that, A.E. Once a very wise old woman told me to do what my heart told me to do. I pass that advice on to you."

Dick wasted no time in interviewing the Shermans, once they came down for breakfast. Taking his tea with him, he joined them at their table, and while they picked at the hearty breakfast Peggy served, Dick asked for their whereabouts on Friday and explained the reasons for his questions.

He found himself watching their faces closely. The young, upwardly mobile urbanites had come to this lodge because of Mr. Wortham's article. This morning they were dressed in their Tilley outfits, their hats hung at the ready on the backs of their dining room chairs. Mr. and Mrs. Charles Sherman, known as

Chuck and Debby, were the picture of first-time visitors to Maine. Under Dick's scrutiny they seemed slightly nervous.

"Exactly what is it you want to know?" Chuck methodically cut his strips of bacon.

"Just a general outline of what you and Mrs. Sherman were doing yesterday morning. And the rest of the day. We think Mr. Fremont was killed sometime midmorning. We're trying to track the whereabouts of everyone at the lodge and the surrounding area."

"We went for a day's hike. The kitchen girl put our lunch up for us and we left about nine-thirty. Well, maybe a little later than that. We took the path around the lake, climbed up near the caves and then took the path down past the camps on the other side, had lunch on a beach near the last camp. Nobody was in it. We took a nap and then hiked over that road marked Rowe Hill and went on into Bryant Pond." Chuck frowned slightly as though he was thinking out the words before he spoke.

"The beach was fun—" Debby giggled.

"He's not interested in that, Deb." Chuck took a more serious approach to the questioning. "We stayed for the rest of the afternoon in Bryant Pond. There were antique stores and used-book stores and a place to eat and look out on Lake Christopher. We had a little wine. Then we had dinner. It was after dark by the time we decided to go back. There's a small taxi service so the man in the restaurant called them for us, and the taxi drove us back to the lodge. It must have been around ten then. We'd hung around the bar longer than we realized. We forgot to tell the lodge we wouldn't be in for dinner."

"I know. I missed you last night." Dick was thoughtful. "In the morning, when you left, do you recall seeing anyone up by the cave path? How high up did you go?"

"I left Debby for ten minutes or so and climbed up. But I never got up to the caves. I was near the ledges, I think."

"Did you notice anyone sitting on the ledges?"

"I don't think so. I was only gone about ten minutes wasn't I, Deb?"

Mrs. Sherman poured herself a second cup of coffee from the small pewter pot Peggy had left on the stand by the table. Then, almost as an afterthought, she poured one for her husband. "That is what you said, dear."

Hmm, thought Dick, slight battle of wills going on here. How long was he gone, and for what reason? Maybe he liked to climb and she didn't. Maybe he had a call of nature. Maybe he'd met Mr. Fremont and had some sort of argument. How much could they have had to do with each other in the few days they'd been at the lodge? The Shermans came on Tuesday. Mr. Fremont came on Wednesday. What was the connection? If there was a connection.

Mrs. Sherman offered Dick coffee, but he shook his head and finished his tea.

Something must have happened up there. He'd try a new tack.

"Did either of you hear anything?"

"Well, we did think we heard someone, once." Debby looked at her husband. "Like something stumbling through the bushes. I let out a yell, I thought it might be a bear. It was probably a deer."

"Probably." Dick looked sternly at the two of them. Why was it so hard for them to meet his eyes?

"You didn't see a person. Just heard a noise?"

"Well, I did think I saw a flash." Debby again seemed to be dragging it out. "Bluish, through the trees. In fact, I said that, didn't I, Chuck? I said there's something blue."

"I guess you did say that. I'd forgotten. Probably a bluejay. She doesn't know a thing about birds, Sheriff."

Dick shrugged. They could give him any title they wanted as long as they answered his questions. Funny, they both seemed to be at odds with each other.

"Either of you have any idea what time this was?" Dick felt as though he was reading Dick and Jane to two errant children.

"Well, we left the lodge about nine-thirty, I guess. And we walked up the path toward the caves, then I decided I'd climb up higher. Debby doesn't like to go too high so she waited for me. I wanted to take a little looksee myself. Then I came back and it was just about then that we heard the noise. We did have a map A.E. had given us, and we were looking at it and deciding whether we'd take the path down toward the camps or take one that was marked to the monument. We decided to go to the other side by the camps."

"And that's when you heard this noise." Dick tried leading them back.

"I guess so, wasn't it, Deb?" Somehow Mr. Sherman didn't seem as positive as he had at first.

"Yes. Then we went down the trail past the other camps on the other side of the lake and on to the road and then to town. Bryant Pond, you know. That's about it."

Dick sighed. "Did you pass anyone on the way along the road?"

"A couple of cars. A jogger. A truck with hay, I guess. I can't remember anything else."

"A jogger? What did he look like? Or she."

"Oh, I'm sure it was a he. I don't know, he had sweats on and he was just ordinary. A truck was going by. He had a headband, I think."

"Would you know him if you saw him again?" Dick already knew the answer. Debby and Chuck Sherman, he had decided, were either extremely obtuse or extremely devious.

Which one, he thought, remains to be seen.

Debby finished the last piece of toast. "I suppose I might know him. But we'll only be here today, we're leaving Sunday."

"Anyone registered at the lodge has to stay around for a few days." For the first time Dick felt in full command.

"But I have to get back to my brokerage house." Charles Sherman was not used to being given orders.

"You might have to identify someone. I'd plan on staying a few more days. You'd better check out your room with A.E. I understand some more people are coming in today. But I'd plan on being here at least until Tuesday, if I were you. And thank you for your information." Dick made a quick exit as Debby started to sputter.

For a moment the couple sat silently. Then Chuck turned on Debby with vehemence.

"I told you to be quiet. Whatever made you have to say we heard anything or saw anything. You just can't shut up, can you?"

"And you couldn't help coming here for our honeymoon, could you? I told you in the beginning I didn't want to come to Maine. Now let's see how you propose to get us out of this mess."

Chapter Nine

At ten o'clock on Saturday morning, Lee and Hod, with A.E. and Motorboat Jones, sat in a screened-in corner of the lodge porch waiting for Dick to finish with the Shermans. In the kitchen Enough prowled around Peggy although he was supposed to be helping her with the vegetables for tonight's dinner. He had tried in a dozen different ways to entice her into the pantry for a quick squeeze, but Peggy, to whom this was old hat, was not feeling in the mood for this green youth today. Her mind was on bigger fish and a date she had made for later this afternoon when she had free time between three and five o'clock. Usually she went up to a room on the third floor that was given over to her during her hours at the lodge, a room A.E. had fixed up with a small white single bed covered with a flounced dotted swiss bedspread and several pillows to match. A dressing table, a large easy chair, and a small radio completed her retreat. Peggy kept a few changes of clothing, her bathrobe, and a small TV set there. The little bathroom on the third floor was hers alone. Only A.E. came up to the tower room to do her accounts. Peggy generally had the floor to herself. Reached by the back stairs, it had once housed four helpers during the days when the lodge did a rushing business, but now there was only Peggy and Enough.

A.E., knowing that Enough should also have a retreat, had taken a storeroom in the old barn and, with the aid of a bedsleeper and some chairs, had given him his own space. She had first considered a second room on the same floor with Peggy, but the girl had pointed out to her that if she did, it was only a matter of time until Enough showed up in her bed.

A.E., thinking of her own apprenticeship in Europe, had laughed and made Enough's arrangements as far from Peggy as possible.

Enough complained to Motorboat, who, on one of the early morning fishing trips, suggested to A.E. that this actually might be a good way to break Enough in. He didn't mention it a second time after A.E. shoved him out of the canoe, and they both ended up in the pond. Luckily they were close enough to shore to save both fishing gear and the can of worms.

"You got an explosive temper there, woman." Motorboat wiped his face and squeezed out his pant legs. "Damned if you don't. Nobody's ever going to want to marry you, you keep doing things like that."

"You keep saying things like that, nobody's going to even get the chance." A.E. walked the canoe in toward the beach and pulled it up, turning it over to drain out the water. "Get hold of the other end, will you. I guess I ought to say I'm sorry. It's just you made me so angry!"

Motorboat sighed. "This is no way to run a relationship."

"Mistake." A.E. snapped. "We don't have a relationship. And if you keep making suggestions about how I run my life, we're never going to have one."

Motorboat, sitting with his feet propped up on the porch railing this Saturday morning, tipped his chair back precariously and smiled to himself as he looked across at A.E. and thought of that early morning dunking a few weeks previously.

Well, he thought to himself, I do seem to be making some progress. It didn't hurt any to have Hod Cole come by and show he knows me, and with the match he's made with Lee Heaward, maybe A.E. will see me in a different light. No, it didn't hurt a bit this morning to come down and pick up Robbie's cart. I'm just going to sit here and see what happens next. The truck can wait.

Lee and A.E. leaned back in the high-backed old Roosevelt rockers, so called because Teddy had once sat in one. They had summered every year on the porch of the lodge since Great-grandfather Fox's day. A.E. and Peggy had fashioned fat blue-and-white canvas cushions for all of these chairs, eight of them in a row across the long porch. Attractive as they were, the seats wore on you after a spell of sitting, and the large striped canvas cushions had brought sighs of relief from the summer visitors. Even Mr. Wortham had admired their qualities.

This morning A.E. wore a clean yellow shirt and her usual balloon jodhpurs. The tall boots had given way to a pair of worn sneakers, and her hair was twisted up in a knot held with a silver clasp that had belonged to Grandmother Fox. Even with A.E.'s individuality of dress, Lee could see what Motorboat admired. There was a bulldog stubbornness here that Lee understood, a reluctance to change and a determination to keep a way of life.

The difference between these two women, one dressed in a 1920s style, the other in simple green culottes and striped T-shirt—the difference was that one had accepted change, the other still fought it.

Lee felt a kinship with A.E. She wanted badly to help, but knew she could not. This was a problem unique to one's self.

Looking at Hod, she knew he read her thoughts, and she settled back in her rocking chair, grateful for this man who had once come to her rescue and changed so much in her own life.

I wonder, she thought, if Motorboat could do that for A.E.?

Hod was talking earnestly to the trucker.

"There's no chance in the world Robbie would commit murder. Swampers never harmed anyone. They might do small things, springing traps, cutting fences, taking a little wood off someone else's land. But before they'd kill they melt away into the forest and swamps. I knew a couple of the old ones. They didn't like the outside world much and because of that people thought they were stupid. They weren't. Maybe they were the smart ones. Lee says Robbie's baskets are museum pieces. Swampers never lived to make old bones. I wouldn't be surprised Robbie sleeps a lot— wherever he feels like settling down. I don't see it as unusual that he slept so long up on that ledge."

"I think you've got it pegged right." Motorboat leaned forward to accept another muffin from A.E.'s plate. "I've heard about Robbie's mother. She walked to town when she needed anything the swamp and the forest couldn't provide. Never would take a ride with anyone. Real independent like. But she sent Robbie to school until the eighth grade. He never fitted in, but she made him do his homework and he passed. And she handed down the basket-making craft. Her father taught her and her grandmother taught her father. Robbie doesn't talk much, but that doesn't mean he's stupid."

"You could be right, Motorboat." Dick joined the four people on the porch. "As far as I can see there was a lot of activity going on up on that mountain. Mr. Fremont started out to go to the caves. Robbie walked up the trail and settled himself in for a nap. The Shermans were out taking a hike and they say they heard a noise and saw something, but they don't know what. Or they aren't telling what. On top of that there must have been the murderer, who took the mallet out of Robbie's pack basket, killed Mr. Fremont, and then replaced the mallet. He, or she, took some awful chances."

"Didn't have any fingerprints, did it?" Hod asked the question.

"Nope, wiped clean, and no way Robbie would do that. So we are pretty sure someone lifted it and cleaned it afterward. Doesn't make much sense, but nothing does."

"Now what?" Hod looked at Dick.

"Now I start looking for other people. The three camps on the other side, maybe someone there saw something. Mrs. Sherman said they saw a jogger. They didn't notice where he went to, they were walking toward town. At least they say they were. And, according to them, they'd never met Mr. Fremont before they came to the lodge."

"I think that's true. He's come here for a long time. This is their first summer, and as far as I know they came from Mr. Wortham's article. The people coming this afternoon all came from this same article. I don't know any of them."A.E. felt her hands trembling.

"Well, I'm off. Got work to do on my Kenworth this morning. I'll drive the cart over to Robbie's. Where did he go?" Motorboat rose.

"I think he walked on back. He said he didn't want to ride, he needed to tell Howard the cart was coming." A.E. folded a napkin around one of Peggy's bran muffins and offered it to the trucker. "Here, for later on."

Motorboat grinned. "Later on'll do."

Dick rose, and A.E., along with Hod, followed him to the cruiser.

"I don't know exactly what to do about Mr. Fremont's things, Dick."

"Just keep that room closed. I can't lock it without a key, but one of the deputies put a seal on the door. I'm going to take another look through it this afternoon, but for right now I want to go over to the other side of the lake and see if anyone in the camps saw anything or anyone. Walter Desmond has a camp over there, hasn't he?"

A.E. nodded. "I think they move up there every summer. Have you seen Old Bill Bannerman?"

"Yes. Now he was up in that area around the same time everyone else was. Says his head hurt, and he went back home. He didn't see anyone, or at least that's what he says. Just sat on a rock and rested for a while and then decided to go back to his camp. That whole mountain was a damn turnpike."

"Maybe he was the noise the Shermans heard." Hod joined in.

"Robbie couldn't have arrived yet, or he was sleeping on the lower ledge, and Old Bill didn't see him. Or he didn't get up that far. He didn't say what rock he was on."

"I believe Robbie, Dick."

"Strangely enough, so do I," the trooper agreed. "Look, I have to check in at home with Frieda. Then I'm going over to the camps on the other side of the pond. I'll be back later this afternoon. Are you feeling any better, A.E.?"

"I made an appointment with Dr. Anna for Tuesday."

"I think Motorboat got your adrenaline moving." Dick ducked a backhanded swipe from A.E. "Save some of that moxie for your guests."

Hod walked back to the porch, leaving A.E. still talking with Dick. He settled himself opposite Lee and looked at her. "You're thinking something, aren't you? Three guesses."

"You might be able to help, Hod. You're good at puzzles. And you know the swamp and the woods. Where do you think Howard came from? Doesn't it seem a little unlikely that a pony would be wandering through a swamp?"

"More than a little unlikely. I've been searching my brain. We don't have gypsies coming through any more. And I haven't heard of anyone hauling horses who broke down and lost any. There's no farms nearby, except Danner's, and they'd know if they lost any stock. There is one old place out past Bill Bannerman's camp. But that's been empty for years. It belongs to someone from Massachusetts, I think. The house is half falling down. The owner comes up to hunt in the fall. I recall I came across it one year when I was hunting in that area. I don't even know if that road is passable past Bill's."

"You might want to tell Dick that." Lee leaned forward.

"Dick just left. What place are you talking about?" A.E. rejoined them.

"There's an old farm beyond Bill's camp. The buildings are in rough shape. But the road branches off near Bill's. He probably wouldn't notice if anyone went in there. I think they just use it for hunting." Hod was thoughtful.

"We really should go now." Lee rose. "It's going to get hotter after last night's rain. I haven't any appointments this weekend but we both have things to do at High Meadows. I'll phone you tomorrow, A.E., and give you some idea of value on the lodge. Sort of a market analysis figure, but you'll find Walter will want a thorough appraisal. You don't have a large mortgage now, so you've plenty of equity."

Hod and Lee left, and A.E., gathering up dishes, joined Peggy in the kitchen.

"Where's Enough?"

"Someplace far away, I hope." The slim blonde giggled. "He is a persistent one. But I'm not about to rob the cradle."

A.E. set the tray down and looked at her kitchen helper. "Peggy—" She hesitated as the girl swung around and confronted her.

"Look, I work for you but I don't need your advice. I can take care of myself. You're good to me, you pay me well, and I'm happy here. For a while. But I'm not here forever. So—thanks. O.K.?"

"O.K." All the things she suspected and wanted to say settled in the back of her mind. She had never been one to mind another's business. But Peggy was so pretty and so vulnerable and so hard. A.E. shook her head and turned away. Déjà vu.

"I'm going upstairs to look over the rooms. I'll put fresh towels in the Shermans' room and make the bed as soon as they go out. Then I'll come down, and we can go over tonight's menu. What do you think about those rosemary biscuits?"

Peggy's attitude changed. "Great. Let's make some without herbs too, and we can use those for your strawberry shortcake. With some of those berries from Denmark you put in the freezer. Remember the day we went picking? That was a fun day, A.E." Suddenly she crossed the room and put her arms around the older woman. "Look, I was rude, I know you care about me, and I'm grateful. But I can take care of myself."

A.E. hugged her back. "Oh, Peggy, please do."

CHAPTER TEN

On this Saturday morning after the storm, Walter Desmond stood contemplating his garden. He was alone at camp, Carol and the children having driven to Boston to shop for school clothes and stay with her mother. If the truth were known, he was glad to be alone. The family had too much togetherness at times, and the camp on Indian Pond, far from being a retreat from his work at the bank, was becoming a haven for noisy teenagers' with their boomboxes. The teenager's appetites were cleaning out the camp refrigerator every weekend.

The last straw had been this past Sunday when they'd consumed a whole cold roast of beef without even asking Carol's permission.

Walter looked at his cabbages marching in diagonal rows across the left-hand side of the garden. He liked planting in diagonal instead of straight rows. Still regimented, but a little different, going off on a different tack. The cabbages were new this year, purchased from the Cooks Garden in Vermont, a type called Salarite—compact almost lettuce-looking plants of medium green. He had started them early in the little greenhouse off the kitchen of their town house and brought them carefully snuggled in their small pots up to the garden at camp. Every year he had planted a garden since they had purchased the camp with Lee Heaward's help ten years ago. The cabbages grew happily, settling in and surpassing even his expectations. They were perfect for the lakeside garden.

And perfect for the woodchucks. Yearly Walter fought a running battle with these creatures. By now, he suspected, they began to watch for him in April, and when he planted in May, they had already decided on their yearly plan of attack. No matter what tactics he tried he always lost some plantings to their appetite for greens.

It's not tactics I need, he thought. That's when you know what the enemy plans. It's strategy—for the unknown. He settled back on his heels, and, picking earwigs off leaves, he dwelt on how those woodchucks changed their tactics yearly. One year it had been lettuce that attracted them, Red Leprechaun, the pink-and-cream leaves with burgundy interiors falling prey to a whole family of the small beasts. Sitting up every so often to watch for Walter's presence (he was convinced) they chewed methodically down the rows. This year they ate cabbages, and Walter was at the point of considering the Great Destroyer as a last resort and one not subscribed to by Carol, who hated to kill anything.

"Look," he had said, filling Carol's gin-and-tonic glass with shaved ice and fitting the little wedge of lime precisely above the hand-cut star on the side of the Waterford crystal goblet. "Look, it's one or the other. I'm in control, or I'm not. Carol, these are woodchucks we're discussing."

The Friday evening drink on the stone porch in front of the camp settled into the usual amicable debate.

"You're not in control." Carol had sipped daintily and looked thoughtfully at this tall, tense man who structured every detail of their lives.

"Bested by a woodchuck. How would that sound at the bankers' convention?" She had giggled and slurped, something he hated, then hastily wiped up the front of her expensive coverall, simple but country chic for their own prescribed Friday evening happy hour.

"Oh, I'm just funnin', honey. Of course you're in control. Get rid of them any way you want. I don't care."

"The electric fence didn't work. The damn things just skin under. The best thing was the radio. That kept them away for a while, until the battery wore out. I think that's probably the best way, except it keeps getting knocked over. If I didn't know better I'd think they know how to turn it off. They don't like the sound, but I'll get them yet." He stared into space.

Carol had been silent. She knew their middle daughter, Celeste, didn't like the sound either. She had told her mother so, and admitted also to turning the radio off in the middle of the night. A typical Desmond, she simply took matters into her own hands and saw no reason to inform her father that she couldn't sleep with the garden music. Boomboxes she related to, not Golden Oldies.

"You take it all so seriously." Carol had picked up the conversation. "I mean, it's just a couple of woodchucks. We can buy vegetables. It's a lot of work to start all those seeds and then transport the plants up here and put them in the garden. I don't care much about it, and I can't come up during the week, with the bridge club and feeding all those teenagers. I really don't know why you bother."

"It's my therapy," Walter had replied. "You just don't understand what's going on in the banks these days. Savings and Loans aren't the old-fashioned banks they used to be. If I can just retreat here to camp on weekends and get my hands in the soil, maybe I can survive all the changes. It seems as though we always need more money. Now it's college expenses coming up this fall—"

"Well, I thought we saved for all that, honey. Haven't we put something away every week ever since we were married?" She had contemplated the hand-cut star in the bottom of her glass, shrewder than she appeared. "You always take care of the money. Don't we have enough for college?"

Walter had sighed. "Everything's gone up. In our tax bracket there aren't many scholarships. Even if the children were smart enough to be eligible."

Secretly, Walter knew the children weren't. When he really thought about it, he knew they took after Carol. Cotton fluff for brains. Partly my own fault, he had thought. I gave them anything they wanted. A big mistake on my part. He had sighed again, reached for Carol's glass to make her a refill, and on his way to the small bar inside the porch doorway, he had taken time to pick a dead leaf off an old rose-scented geranium that sat on a low wicker table.

Now, resting on his heels beside the garden on this Saturday morning, he remembered the conversation with Carol. How did I ever get into this position? How, my boy, are you going to work your way out?

Walter loved a challenge. Woodchucks notwithstanding, he always intended to win. And he would beat them yet.

Standing up, he looked at his watch and decided the garden did not need attention at this moment. He might decide to use the bomb a little later when the woodchucks were taking their afternoon naps. Right now he would walk up toward the caves. He had jogged this morning early, running along the lake road and then up along Rowe Hill Road, one of the two directions he made a choice of each morning. But it had been misty, still damp from the rain the night before and humid. Now, with the sun out and the warmth of the late morning, he decided he would walk up the path leading toward the lower trail going up to the mountaintop. He had two mornings off from the bank this week, yesterday and today. Today, Saturday, only the drive-up window was open. He looked at his watch and judged whether or not he could walk the path in half an hour, going up at least to the intersection coming up from Bill Bannerman's camp. It would give him just time enough to see if anyone else had been up that path this morning.

He took the shore path along the pond, following what must have been the Indian trail, then began to climb upward toward the ledges and the caves. The ascent was gradual, not as steep as the trail coming up on the other side from Indian Lodge. About a third of a mile along, Walter came to the junction of the three trails. One led to the top of the mountain with the so-called ledges and the caves. One led along the mountainside, horizontally below the upper trail, and the third led off to the right to a woods road leading to Bill Bannerman's cabin. Beyond this was the old farm Hod had mentioned to Lee. From Bill's another road led out to Rowe Hill.

The banker, perspiring in the gathering heat, followed the trail to the top and ten minutes later came out above the ledge Robbie has chosen, just below the entrance to the cave where Mr. Fremont had been working. Walter turned, looking down at the pond, the waters sequin splattered in the sun.

He saw, as Robbie had seen, the lodge lawn, the meadow beyond with its entrance to the hardwood stand, and around the corner the end of the lake reaching into the swamp. This time of year the marshes were green and gold. Goldenrod and hardhack were in bloom, along with great masses of purple loosestrife, a setting for a Vivian Akers oil.

A serene sight with no hint of murder. Walter sighed and sat down. There was a magic here, high above the lake, a magic the Indians knew when they chose this valley for a gathering place. A magic that might have sent their shamans to pray high above the valley in the caves, for they believed that heights held secret strengths. And they needed strength, in the face of the encroaching peoples who were infiltrating their land. Could Mr. Fremont have found a clue here? Something to show that the Indian men of magic did pray in these caves?

Walter drew a long breath. Superstition, pure and simple. He only believed in what he could see. In the real world, one made decisions for survival. Banks and people, it was all the same. You had to survive. If someone was hurt, that was not his fault. He had to look at the overall picture, not the individual. Why had everything become so complicated? This past year he had found himself in an almost untenable situation. He wished he could follow the old trails over the mountain and into the past. No one would really miss him. Carol would survive; the children saw him only as a background figure that gave them money and food when they had a need. He provided shelter and seldom interfered with their lives. His contact with his children was through their mother. He preferred it that way. So who would miss him? Maybe just one person. Maybe.

Walter stiffened. Below him came the sound of footfalls. Someone was coming up the path. Instinct told him to fade back into the cave, but an out-of-breath Dick Eggleston clambered up onto the ledge and dropped down beside him before Walter could move.

"Well, surprise. I didn't expect to meet you. This saves me a trip down to your camp. Do you climb up here often?" Dick was puffing.

"Seldom, as a matter of fact. I'm surprised to see you too, Dick. I had about forty minutes for a walk before lunch, and I thought I'd come and see this place. There was a lot of talk around town yesterday. I thought maybe you'd have the paths cordoned off."

"No. As far as we can tell, he was killed where we found him, right where the hardwood stand meets the meadow at the bottom of the trail from the lodge. We think he was returning from the cave, but we don't know why. A.E. says he usually spent most of the day up there. He was booked in at the lodge."

"Yes, I saw her at the bank yesterday afternoon." Walter offered his water bottle to Dick. "You're still puffing."

Dick laughed. "I could be in better shape. What were you doing yesterday morning?"

"We're up at camp for the summer. I get up early and spend some time in the garden. Then I either take a walk or run. I have some vacation time from the bank. This past week I've just been going in for a few hours in the afternoon."

"Where did you go yesterday?"

"Around the lake road and then up the first path to the confluence. I thought I'd take the trail over toward Bill Bannerman's, then back to Rowe Hill and down to camp, but I noticed one shoe was not feeling right, and so I turned back the way I came. I cooled down on the edge of the lake path and tried to work it out, never had a rock catch in a sneaker before like that one, but I could see I'd have to change shoes. So I went back to camp and changed shoes and walked out on the main road for a ways."

"Did you see anyone?"

"A young couple as I remember. And a hay truck. Yes, I think it may have been from Danner's farm. That's all."

"The couple, do you recall what they looked like?"

"I don't think so, I don't pay much attention when I'm running. I have my earphones on and the radio going, you know. Oh, they looked sort of British. Tilley outfits?"

"That would be the Shermans. They're booked in at the lodge. They remember seeing you, too, so that checks. So you never got up to the caves?"

"No. I usually wouldn't run uphill to them, anyway. When I'm walking, that's the only time I would go uphill to the cave or ledge area."

"Well, I guess that's all I need to know right now. I know where to find you. Who's in the other camps?"

"No one permanently. The owners only come once in a while. The economy I guess. I hear one may go up for sale. We usually have a neighborhood arrangement to look out for each other's camps. I've only seen the others twice so far this year. We are pretty much alone on our side. I admit I don't mind."

"Banking must be kind of stressful, right now." Dick, who put most of his small savings into mutual funds, looked at the tall, tense man. "That's why I like my job, I'm outside most of the time. But I admit when there's a murder I'd trade my job for yours."

"Don't be too sure." Walter sounded wistful. "I should be getting on back."

Dick nodded. "I'm going to explore here a bit. I wonder what he might have found. Or seen. Something made him come back down toward the lodge before his usual time."

"I've no idea. He was probably just a senile old man, wishful that he'd found an Indian cache." Walter's voice was brittle. He turned and started down the mountain.

Dick remained seated, looking down at the pond. Something was bothering him, and he suddenly realized that either Walter Desmond was a slow jogger or he had taken much longer than necessary to change sneakers. There was a long span of time between early morning, when Walter had left his camp to run, and the time that the Shermans thought they had seen him along Rowe Hill Road. Someone did not seem to be telling the truth. Or they had no sense of time.

That someone could be Mr. Fremont's killer.

CHAPTER ELEVEN

Near two o'clock on Saturday afternoon Lee and Hod ate a late lunch on the screened porch at High Meadows. They had spoken little since leaving the lodge on Indian Pond that morning, each lost in thought over the murder. For murder it definitely was. The medical examiner's full report had just come in to Dick Eggleston, and he had phoned both A.E. and Hod as soon as he'd gotten down off the mountain and found Dr. Anna's message awaiting him.

"Hod, I have two deputies in on this, but I know how much you helped Reed Jamison last year when Lee was threatened. You know these mountains as well as anyone in Oxford County. Could I come by in the next hour and talk with you? A couple of things bother me."

Hod, holding the phone in one hand, encircled Lee with his free arm.

"Dick Eggleston wants to know can he come by now? I might get to play detective again."

Lee nodded. "I never realized how much you enjoyed it until it was all over last year. Certainly he can. I'll put some water on to boil, he likes black tea, not coffee. Ask him if he's had lunch."

Hod relayed the message, assured Dick of a sandwich, and thoughtfully looked at the smiling, curly-haired woman who had become a large part of his life.

"Last year wasn't fun, Lee. The bear came too close. But, you're right. I do like puzzles, and this looks to be a good one. I wish Reed hadn't gone to Boston. Dick's a fine trooper, one of our best, but his mind's on Frieda right now. He told me she's had a hard time carrying this child." Hod's eyes suddenly seemed far away.

Lee covered a lean brown hand with her own. Only once had he told her the story of his own young wife who had died giving birth to a child. Lee had lost her own husband in a car accident. They sat silently, no words needed.

Finally Hod spoke.

"I never told you. They're buried on a small island in the Androscoggin. It connects with a bridge to the mainland. Her family are all buried there—the cemetery goes back to the 1700s. They had to ferry them out by raft the first hundred years. The island's right in mid river, above a set of rapids. The bridge comes off both ends. I think she was the last person buried there. I haven't set foot in that graveyard for years. Thinking of Dick makes me remember. Time I paid a visit there."

Lee squeezed his hand. It was quiet, with only the sounds of the warblers in the sweet olive and the hummingbirds darting in and out of the trumpet vine to disturb the stillness. Under the table Kate Gordon stretched her front paws and touched the man's feet, and a tanned hand absently petted the black-and-gold setter.

Please, God, thought Lee, I have not prayed in a long while. Please bring Frieda and the baby safely through.

Aloud, she spoke gently to the man beside her. "If you want, I'll go with you."

Dick arrived shortly, showing signs of strain. He had been up late and risen early, spending the hours in between talking with Frieda. Dr. Anna had called in and reassured both of them, but a cloud of doubt still caused persistent gloom in the small house. His private life was beginning to affect his job, and Dick needed to talk with someone outside the troopers' barracks, someone like Hod Cole who had gained a reputation for solving puzzles. Dick knew Reed Jamison slightly. He knew the respect Reed had for the timberman. Dick decided he would ask for a little help. Right now, he needed all he could get.

Lee left the two men alone on the porch. She called the setter and walked to the pasture to bring the horses inside for their afternoon naps. The sun was hot now, the temperature up to nearly 90 degrees, and the box stalls were cool. Native and Musette dipped their noses in the cool water buckets as Lee shot the bolts on their stall doors. With Kate at her heels, she returned to the house. The answering service light was on, and she returned Meg's call. Then she rejoined the men on the porch.

Hod had spread a map across the top of the wooden porch table. Pots of red geraniums held down each end. One of his extensive collection of Maine county maps, this one showed the Bryant Pond area with Indian Mountain and Indian Pond. Present roads were marked along with old county roads and trails. Tiny squares indicated old homesteads existing in 1862, tiny dots indicated schools and churches. This was not like the large 1862 wall map that hung in the barn tack room, now Hod's domain, but a smaller replica of the Oxford County area. Hod's pencil tapped the area around Indian Mountain.

"There's the old trail, up around the lakeshore, that's supposed to be the old Indian route. That square is an old farm, just about on the site of Indian

Lodge. Here's the trail coming from Rowe Hill Road in by the camps. They aren't on this map because they didn't exist then."

"What's that?" Lee, who studied maps weekly in her real estate rounds, was not familiar with this one.

"I think that might be where Robbie's cabin is now. See, it's all swamp down this end of the lake and there are several squares in through here. I'd guess it might be one of the Swamper settlements."

"You mean there was a settlement there?" This was news to Dick.

"Probably seven or eight families. That was in the 1800s. They died out or moved away, and all the houses rotted or burned. Houses burned in those days because of the way the chimneys were attached. Some of them had wooden chimneys"

"Did you know Robbie's mother?" This part of Hod's background was new to Lee.

"Slightly. She died right after her father died. They were both basketmakers. In fact most of the Swampers made baskets. Kept bees, collected wild herbs, kept pretty much to themselves except for when they came into town with their baskets. Robbie's cabin is the last one there except for one other, and that's gone now, I think. Over the trail, and out past Bill Bannerman's camp was another old farm. It may have been one of the Swampers moved out and set-tled out there, fewer mosquitoes, maybe. Local lore says lots of the Swampers died from swamp fever."

"So Robbie is the last." Dick's pencil traced the lines coming out of the swamp and up toward the peak of the mountain. "This trail comes up, then joins the other two, and one goes to the mountain caves and one runs parallel to the top trail. Is that right? I was up where they joined this morning. I met Walter Desmond up on the ledges."

"They call the place where these three trails join the Confluence. This one goes to the old farm past Bill Bannerman's. Walter Desmond up there too, was he? It's getting to be a right busy place, that mountain."

"That's what I'm beginning to think." Dick looked closer at the map. "Does it show the caves?"

"There's one word here: ledges. If you read the history of the county you'll find they speak of roads, buildings, a few natural formations, but not much about caves and ledges. More about the minerals and gems. There's a book written about Mollyockett that mentions the trails running down through the area, then down the Androscoggin to Sebago and the ocean. There were a few gathering places of note. One was supposed to be along the shores of Indian Pond. We call the paths we follow the old Indian trails. But the Swampers could have made several of them themselves in their search for ash for their baskets, or when they gathered herbs or hunted.

"Funny thing," Hod continued. "They didn't eat much game. You could almost call them vegetarians. And they didn't live to be very old. Not much over fifty, any of them. Robbie actually is older than his family history says he ought to be."

"How do you know all that?" Lee searched Hod's face.

"Oh, I've known him for several years. Met him in the woods on and off. That's why I know he'd never lie. He might not tell all the truth, but he'd never lie. And he'd never kill. Strange, though. I don't think he's told us all he knows about Howard."

Lee interrupted. "I've called several horse people. No one has heard of a lost pony. I'm beginning to think he might not be from around here."

"What keeps going through my mind is the thought he might have some connection with Mr. Fremont. Doesn't it seem rather unusual that a man is murdered up on that mountain and a pony is lost in the swamp below? Someone has to own that pony. He got here somehow." Dick stared into his tea cup.

"Well, if it's advice you're asking, I'd suggest we take a good look around the area where Robbie said he found him, then see if we can find that old road to the farm beyond Bill's. That's the only place in the area you haven't checked. There may be nothing there, but someone could have camped out there and may have been on the mountain. All sorts of people hiking and camping out this month." Hod rolled up the map and put it back in a small metal case.

"That's exactly what I had in mind. By any chance you want to go with me, Hod?"

"By any chance the moon coming up tonight? Just wait until I change my boots."

Lee put a hand on Dick's arm as Hod disappeared into the kitchen.

"I'm glad you asked him. Dick, there is something that puzzles me. Howard is not an ordinary pony. I think he's a Pony of America and may be trained for more than riding."

"What do you mean?"

"Well, I've had horses all my life. And I watched him with Robbie. Those two communicated. They could read each other's minds. Some people can do it with animals. A.E. can. I can do it with my mare. And Robbie can do it with Howard. I could see that."

"Minds? Lee—"

"No, Dick, this is not fantasy. It really can happen. The thing is, if you owned a pony as smart as Howard, wouldn't you be out searching for him?"

Dick looked keenly at this woman whose mind seemed to have zeroed in on something both he and Hod had missed.

"Yes," he answered slowly." I guess I would. Except if—"

"Except if what?" Lee leaned forward.

"Except if I was dead."

CHAPTER TWELVE

Half an hour later, traveling the road in toward Old Bill's cabin in Hod's jeep, Dick noted the driving had not improved. He had left the cruiser at the courthouse, relieved that Hod's four-wheel-drive would probably make the trip easier and less noticeable in case they did find anyone at the old farm. That is, if it still existed. If it had not been a Saturday, Dick would have made a call to the Woodstock town office to find who owned the property they were searching for, but now he would have to wait until Monday and regular office hours.

"Shall we stop by to check Bill?" Hod had been thinking intently as they drove along.

"Good idea. I told him to stick around. He and Alexander were great buddies, according to A.E., and I don't see him killing the minister. His reaction when I told him sure wasn't faked. He's pretty badly shaken up over the man's death. Could be he's turned up something."

Hod stopped at the fork in the road. "We're going to the right?"

"Yup. We'll see Bill and then take that left branch. It sure looks closed in, but we'll try it. We may have to walk a good part of the way, if your map was right."

"Those old maps weren't too far wrong. Here we are." Hod braked in time to miss a partridge shooting up from the spruces near Bill's cabin.

On the porch, Bill leaned back in his chair in the exact same spot he'd occupied the day before. Alexander's death had saddened the ex-teacher and ex-convict. It had taken him a long while on Friday to accept the fact that one of his few friends had been killed. He'd pulled on his boots and spent the rest of the daylight hours going over the mountain trail, looking in at the caves and slowly walking down the other side of the mountain to the yellow tape marking the area where Alexander's body had been found. He trudged back up to the caves again, sat for a while on Robbie's ledge, and watched the valley below, wondering what the basketmaker might have seen.

Bill had seen the help leave the lodge, Peggy driving her small Volkswagen and Enough wheeling his bicycle up the dirt road to Rowe Hill Road where it was then downhill all the way to Motorboat's small house in the village. It was nearly dark by then, and Bill knew he should get off the mountain. His old feet did not have the sureness of youth. He met no one coming down from the caves, yet he had a feeling someone or something watched him as he reached the bottom and turned toward his own camp. Safe from the darkness, he poured two fingers of Jack Daniels from an untapped bottle, and, as an afterthought, shot the bolt on the door. Saturday morning he had a blazing headache, and it had taken several hours and two pots of coffee before he felt better. Now, after a meager lunch of a tuna fish sandwich with lettuce and more coffee, he was leaning back thinking through yesterday when Hod and Dick raised the partridge and came rattling into the yard.

"Back again." Bill's voice was not hospitable. "Hod Cole, it's been years since I've seen you. I heard about you last summer. Seems you're getting to be quite a detective."

Hod ignored what seemed to be sarcasm. "I'm sorry about your friend, Bill. We have another puzzle, maybe you can help."

Bill leaned forward. He was older than Hod, but in a way the two men were alike—laconic, quiet, and economical in their motions and designs. They both had spent years reading, their knowledge was eclectic, and they both had a love for these Maine woods and mountains. Bill had drawn more inward in the last few years. Hod had expanded his horizons with the encouragement and caring of Lee. Between the two men was a mutual, but guarded, respect.

"Bill, do you know anyone who's lost a pony?" Dick sat down on the edge of the porch, brushing dirt off his boots. "Robbie, the basketmaker, found one in the swamp, least he says he did. Caught in a fence. And you probably don't know, Robbie's a suspect of sorts. It was his mallet killed Alexander Fremont."

"I heard. That's a mistake, Dick. Robbie would never kill anyone." Bill got up and started inside. "Either of you want some coffee? I have a fresh pot."

Dick, a tea drinker, shook his head, but Hod accepted and followed the older man into the camp.

"It's a real neat camp you got here, Bill. Reminds me of mine in Sumner."

"I heard you closed it up for a while."

Hod rarely discussed his personal life. He saw no reason to discuss this with Bill.

Carrying their thick mugs, the men returned to the porch. Dick made short work of explaining their visit.

"I'm not checking on you, Bill. We want to take a look at that old farm, if there's anything left of it, on the left-hand turn. Do you know who owns it, or if they're there?"

"Town office could tell you that. Saturday, though, isn't it? I think it's someone from Massachusetts. They came up some years ago, when I first came in the summer. But I haven't seen them recently. Doesn't seem to be much of a trail there anymore. I expect deer hunters might know." He looked at Hod.

Hod smiled. "Reputations die hard. It's been years since I've been in there. We thought we'd drive, or walk in today. It's the one place on the mountainside hasn't been pretty well looked over. Dick and the deputies have been all along the paths and they've checked anyone who was in the area."

"You care to come, Bill?" Dick hesitated before asking, then decided it could do no harm.

"No, I guess not. I'd just slow you up." The older man readjusted his weight in the hickory chair and waved one gnarled hand at them. "You go along. If you don't come out in a couple of hours I'll figure you found somebody."

"It might not be a bad idea to think along those lines." Dick wondered how much help Bill really could be in an emergency. "Hardly seems likely anyone's in there, no signs of travel. But we'll take a look."

Ten minutes later, Hod and Dick, still in the car, came to an opening and faced what remained of a farmhouse and surprisingly, what looked like a fairly well kept barn. The grounds about the house were grown up, but the dirt driveway, instead of petering out as they had expected, widened on each side and gave the look of having been used recently. The old white farmhouse leaned, one side had clapboards off, and someone had put tar paper over the sheathing and evidently prepared for some reconstruction. The chimney had been rebricked and mortared and the porch, although sporting some rotten boards, supported an old armchair. Someone obviously had been here recently.

"It looks like somebody's house." Dick mounted the rickety steps and knocked on the front door. "Maybe we'll get lucky."

Hod moseyed around the side toward the barn, and while Dick waited for an answer to his knock, Hod's keen eyes took in a four-wheel Toyota and a horse trailer parked in the bushes on one side of the barn. He walked slowly, his eyes shifting from side to side. Somehow there was a feeling of malevolence in this out-of-the-way spot. Hod was attuned to trouble. He walked warily.

Dick, getting no answer at the door, came down off the porch to join Hod. They both stood without speaking, looking at the trailer, which had been disconnected from the car, and backed into the bushes. The open side faced the two men. Carefully, Dick swung up into the horse trailer and looked around.

"The haykeeper's here, still has some in it, and part of a bale here in the front. Must have been only one horse. Here's his rope, but no halter. No way to tell how long this trailer's been here."

Hod was looking at the ground. "Well, it rained heavy last night. If this rig came in this morning they'd be tracks. Don't seem to be any, so it came in before then. No hoofprints about on the ground, either. Been here some time,

I'd say." Hod's voice reverted to its Maine accent.

"Toyota now," he said, peering in the window, "No keys, doors unlocked. Seems a tad queer. No answer at the house?"

"No. If he brought a horse trailer, you'd reckon he brought a horse. We better look in the barn, Hod."

Hod was still the tracker. "Well, that don't necessarily follow. He could have hauled something else in that trailer, I suppose. But with a haykeeper and some extra hay and the smell of it, I'd guess he did bring a horse. Question is, where is he, and where's the horse?"

"That," said the trooper, "is what I aim to find out."

They approached the house again. Again Dick knocked, but there was still no answer. He turned the doorknob gently and the old Victorian door opened to the interior.

"No squeak," remarked Hod, eyes flickering over the room. "Someone keeps it oiled."

The interior was bare. The front rooms were empty with peeling wallpaper and scarred floors. It had been years since the Massachusetts family had spent a summer there. But the kitchen showed occupancy. The old range connected to the chimney with new stovepipe, and the table was clean. A small single bed was made up by the side of the room. On the table beside it was a Coleman lantern, some folded pieces of clothing, and a box of crackers. The cupboard by the stove revealed three boxes of macaroni and cheese mix, and a pot on the stove, when Hod lifted the cover, revealed the dried remains of a meal. He sniffed, wrinkled his nose, and commented, "Smells like it's been here a while."

Dick opened the door to the pantry. "There's a cooler in here. Someone planned to stay for a few days." He opened the top and backed away from the smell.

"Smells like it's been here a while, too. The ice is all gone. That meat's pretty high. Now, why would you bring a cooler all the way in here and then not use the supplies before the ice ran out?"

"Another thing." Hod stood looking down at the bedside table. Here's a couple of Ace bandages. The kind you wear if you have a bad ankle. He might have had a bad foot. So he might not be able to walk far."

The two men looked at each other.

"You know, it's so simple it can't be right. Suppose you can't walk far, but you have to get around somehow. You don't want to use an ATV or a mountain bike and let everyone hear you. What kind of transportation would you use, Dick, that wouldn't make too much noise?"

"A horse. But why in hells bells would I drag him all the way up here from Massachusetts? Why wouldn't I rent one here?" The trooper was overwhelmed with this new development. He shook his head.

"This is a little bit crazy, Hod. What is this man-if it is a man—doing up here anyway?"

"That's exactly what I want to know. And what's it got to do with Mr. Fremont or Howard? Actually, there's probably a reasonable explanation, and it doesn't have anything to do with either of them. Only one thing—" Hod paused.

"And that is?"

"Where is he? He brings up all this food and doesn't eat it and here's his horse trailer and no horse. I think you ought to call in this license number to Massachusetts and find out who owns that Toyota. And maybe we better get a search party out to find him. And the horse."

"That's just what I'm going to do." The trooper followed Hod out of the house and stood looking about the yard.

"We haven't searched the barn yet. One thing puzzles me more than anything else, though. See that, Dick?"

The trooper stared. "That trailer hasn't any license plate. Neither does the Toyota. How come? They had to have license plates to drive up here. What kind of people we dealing with, Hod?"

The timberman's eyes narrowed. "Not what I'd call friendly. In fact, there's something here I don't like at all. We've got a missing horse and a missing person. Chances are we'll find the horse if Robbie hasn't already found him. But I'm betting when we find the person he isn't going to be alive."

CHAPTER THIRTEEN

The barn revealed no secrets. Cobwebs hung from corners like crepe paper decorating a dance hall, windows were coated with dust and hay screenings from years past. Nothing had walked through the cavernous spaces recently. Hod and Dick brushed spiderwebs to left and right as they walked across the dusty barn floor and looked into the small adjoining shed. Smaller animals might have frequented the lower regions—raccoon and skunk droppings attested to that—but no larger creature, man nor beast, had entered. No clues here.

Dick wrote down the model and any serial numbers he could find on the Toyota and the horse trailer. With Hod at the wheel, they backtracked down the woods road. They spent a few minutes telling Bill what they'd discovered and then returned to the sheriff's office for Dick to pursue matters further. Hod, reflecting on what they had seen, drove slowly back to High Meadows.

"Lee, why would you bring a horse and trailer up to Maine from Massachusetts? Give me some reasons." Hod sipped iced tea with his feet up on the side railing of the screened porch.

Lee, who had produced the farm's famous iced tea the moment she saw Hod's tired face, placed a plate of oatmeal cookies on the little homemade wooden table that sat between their two old Boston rocking chairs.

"Many reasons. There could have been a scheduled trail ride. Or maybe I had children coming up later. Or I might have been going to sell the horse. Or I was coming up myself for a few weeks and wanted to have my own horse to ride. A lot of summer people bring their horses. Any of those reasons make sense."

"For someone else, they do. Maybe not for this person, though. I think he, or she, had a bad foot. There were bandages on the table. I think they needed transportation so they figured to ride to wherever they were going."

"Then why not bring an ATV? It doesn't eat anything, it should be easier to transport. It will go most anywhere." Lee sounded puzzled.

"We thought of that. Dick came up with the reason, and·I was right behind him. Too much noise. No, wherever this person wanted to go, if that theory is correct, he didn't want any noise."

Lee broke a cookie in half and sat contemplating which half she liked best.

"A horse might not make much noise, but he makes hoofprints. And once in a while a pile of manure."

"Yep, that's true. We haven't really looked carefully at the ground on those trails. I wasn't thinking horse until I saw that trailer. Although, Lee, there's something else. You could wrap the hooves."

"That's a lot of trouble." Lee sat up straight and stopped rocking.

"You really don't want anyone to hear you if you do that. So the reason has to be pretty important."

"Exactly. Now we have a pony caught in a fence. And we have a Toyota and a horse trailer out at that old farm. But no warm bodies of man or beast. And indication someone who was coming back didn't come back. So maybe the pony is the horse who didn't return. But—"

"Where's the man?" Lee interrupted.

"Exactly." Hod sipped thoughtfully. "Exactly. Where's the man? And does he have anything to do with Mr. Fremont? And is Howard the lost horse? Although we call him a pony. You know what, Lee, I'm going to take a nap. It was hot out there on that farm. Maybe I'll take a shower first and scrub off the cobwebs. You wouldn't want to join me?"

Lee smiled and rose from her rocking chair. "In the middle of the afternoon? What took you so long to ask?"

CHAPTER FOURTEEN

Peggy had worked steadily all day since arriving at the lodge. Saturdays were the most demanding days in the kitchen. A.E. was famous for her evening buffet. As much as she disliked being invaded by guests, she kept great grandfather Fox's tradition of good Maine food. Occasionally she added a recipe she had learned in France, but tonight the menu was country Maine.

Today three couples and one single would be booked in by noon. Peggy would check the rooms early, seeing to fresh linen and towels and clean baths. A.E. would go up later and inspect and place small miniature bouquets of wildflowers on the old twig bedside tables and the marble countertops in the bathrooms. Big fluffy white towels made up for the shortage of hot water. Bed linens were edged with lace, and starched white pillowcases covered the four goosedown pillows at the head of every bed. Cakes of Crabtree and Evelyn wild rose soap sat in wicker baskets along with tiny bottles of shampoo and hand lotion. Later, if anyone wanted, tea would be brought up on old wicker trays and placed by the door after a discreet knock.

Great-grandfather Fox would have been proud of his great-granddaughter. Indian Lodge had never lost its old-fashioned ambiance. Mr. Wortham had not been wrong.

Now, early on Saturday afternoon, the salad greens were washed, and A.E. had finished the desserts: Indian pudding and chocolate mousse and big, fluffy biscuits for the strawberry shortcake bases. Everything was prepared as much as possible ahead of time and now, at two-thirty, Peggy sprinted for her third-floor room and a quick bath. The old bathtub had a chromium shower ring above it, but it was unworkable, and Peggy sloshed water in the tub, gave herself a quick all over with a spring-scented freshener, and pulled on a simple cotton shift. She fitted her feet into low sneakers, first coated with powder, no socks, and tied her long blonde hair up with a scarf. This was all in a matter of minutes. She was used to running by a clock, and there was a place and an appointment she meant to keep within the limits of her two hours off from work. She moved down the backstairs and across the lawn so rapidly that Enough, positioned behind one of the log pillars on the end of the side porch, nearly missed seeing her pass.

She was entering the woods when he slid off the porch and followed. The hardwood stand was still cordoned off. Peggy followed a minor path that would rejoin the main trail winding up toward the ledges. Her sneaker-clad feet made no sound, and Peggy, who jogged daily and was an avid basketball player, had no trouble with the upward incline of the path.

You might almost think she was familiar with this mountain.

Enough, in fairly good shape for a fourteen-year-old, still consumed too many pies and donuts with Motorboat. He began to regret his mission. He had tried to track Peggy on previous occasions, but she had always lost him, and he was beginning to think maybe she knew she was being shadowed. This time he was closer than ever before, and he was determined to find out where she disappeared to on Saturday afternoons. If he had any thought of getting seriously involved with Peggy, he had to know his rival.

Enough was a dreamer. He had two goals: one to race at the New Hampshire International Speedway, and the other to have a liaison with Peggy. At fourteen, one dreams. Enough's head often did not follow his feet.

Thinking about all this, he realized Peggy had vanished. There was no sign of her when he reached the first ledge and, looking upward, no sign on the second ledge. She might be in the caves. He turned at the intersection and climbed upward, but a cursory glance showed them empty, and Enough, out of breath, retreated below to Robbie's seat. He looked at the valley below, scanned the woods, but there was no Peggy. On the trail going down toward the camps there were no gaps, it was all trees, and by now Enough had to acknowledge he had lost his quarry.

Peggy, wise in the ways of teenage boys, knew Enough was behind her. She also knew her stride was more than a match for his and that she would elude him within ten minutes. While he was snatching a breather in front of the caves, she was long gone on a connecting path, almost obscured from the main path and running parallel to the mountaintop. In a few moments she would be at a small oak grove, backed against a stone wall where there had once been a house. The cellar hole traces still remained. In the springtime there would be lilies of the valley and lilacs. This mountain had been cleared in the 1800s, and the view across the valley must have been spectacular. Two old oaks had dropped acorns, and a small tree backed against part of the stone wall. Peggy, still moving fast, passed the house site and followed the stone wall to its corner. She sank down, out of sight. The moss here covered an area of almost half an acre. The afternoon sunlight filtered down through the oak leaves. It was a natural resting place, a green velvet couch. A special place for Peggy. And for her partner.

Today he was late. Peggy always made it a prerequisite of an affair that her hours must be observed. Meetings must be where she wished, at the time she wished, and under her guidelines. Peggy's time was money, and these were business arrangements. Above all was the rule of a closed mouth.

Peggy and Dr. Anna Easton had one thing in common. They both knew the value of the unspoken word.

"Sorry, there was someone stumbling about on the trail below. I had to be sure I was out of sight while he went by. That boy from the lodge, Enough. Peggy, I told you I thought he was too nosy." the man folded his body onto the moss beside her and took long breaths. "This whole thing is beginning to get out of hand." He sighed.

"Well, I don't know who killed Mr.Fremont, or what's happening, but your plans shouldn't have to change. I don't think anyone knows what's going on. I listened this morning when that Hod Cole and that real estate woman were on the porch."

"What were they saying?"

"Well, you know Hod Cole doesn't think Robbie did it. He thinks he was framed. And A.E. and that real estate woman agree. Motorboat doesn't think Robbie did it either."

"Motorboat are you still—?"

"That little episode was finished a long time ago. And he never talks. Besides I actually think he's beginning to be sweet on A.E. But he's smart, don't be fooled by the way he looks."

"There's nothing to do now but wait. I think it will die down as so many incidents tend to—they'll never find the connection, and in a year or so we can go ahead with our plans. There're beaches in the world you can disappear on forever. With that amount of money we can go anywhere." The man looked thoughtful. They sat in silence.

"I really should know where it is." Peggy looked up at him. "In case anything should happen to you."

The man sighed and shook his head. "No. Not yet. I have to move it one more time and then I'll show you the spot. In the eyes of the world I have no connection with this and neither do you. So let's leave it at that. Come here."

As they moved together on the mossy bed, Peggy suddenly giggled.

"What's so funny?"

"You, you foolish man. No connection? But you are the connection. That's why this has all happened. You are the connection."

CHAPTER FIFTEEN

For at least another hour and a half, Enough walked back and forth along the trails, depressed at his failure to find Peggy. I just don't have a chance with her, he thought. She always starts along the same path, then she disappears. She's always back at the lodge by five, so she can't go too far. I'm sure she's meeting someone.

He kicked two stones off the pathway ahead of him and practiced some swear words. He had been accumulating them recently in case he found a way to incorporate them into his speech. Life was sure a piss.

Enough realized he was off the main path. Somehow he had sidetracked— courses of old trails snaked through the woods but led nowhere. Some were impassable—they had reverted to heavy brush and tree growth—a few were still used by animals. This was a deer trail, and from the smell of it there must be a dead one nearby. Enough sniffed, then looked down at the ground. The Indian monument was in this area, a stone cache with part of an iron fence surrounding. No one came here any more. In fact it was so grown in now that Enough had a hard time pushing his way through the brush. In front of him two branches seemed broken off, but his eyes were not searching. He was following his nose.

Two coyotes digging at the edge of the pile of stones dissolved into the woods as Enough emerged from the bushes.

The smell was strong now. Enough hesitated, but curiosity triumphed. He looked carefully at the stone cache. Just a pile of stones.

And what looked like a foot.

"Jesum Crow." He shivered. If the foot was connected—he didn't want to consider the possibility. All he wanted to do was get back to the safety of the lodge. Let someone like Dick Eggleston or Motorboat return to explore what might be on the other end of that foot. A possibility Enough didn't want to deal with at the moment. All thoughts of Peggy and her suitor were wiped from his mind. This was an emergency situation.

Enough turned and started backtracking. Parting bushes to find the path, he suddenly ran into a wall of flesh. Hands spun him around, bent his arms behind his back, and in a minute cloth covered his eyes. There was no sound, no warning, but whoever it was must have seen his reaction to the foot sticking out of the cache.

And probably knew who it was in the cache. Probably had put him or her there. Enough struggled, but his captor was stronger and as he was spun around and headed back down the track the fourteen-year-old suddenly knew this was serious. His mouth was bound now, but there was no sound from his captor except heavy breathing.

There was a good chance he was not going to see the lodge again. Ever.

There was no conversation. Once Enough, sobbing, tried to ask a question, but his mouth was jammed with more cloth. And a blow to his head left him reeling.

His abductor pushed him forward, jerked him upright when he stumbled, and moved ahead. It was evident he had a destination in mind.

Enough began to hope. If he'd been going to be killed, it should have happened at the beginning. Maybe he was being taken someplace, maybe hidden. He hoped there would be at least water, he was thirsty by now. And he knew that someone was bound to miss him. Not at the lodge—it was Saturday and he was finished at three, and that was when he'd followed Peggy. Not at home—for Motorboat had decided to run to Connecticut for parts and would be late returning. Besides, Enough knew he liked to fish with A.E. early Sunday mornings, and he might leave the house without waking the boy up. If he did get back from Connecticut. So Enough might not actually be missed until Monday. When he didn't show up at the lodge at eight-thirty, then someone might miss him.

But not before.

The boy shivered. This was no fantasy of the mind, no speeding down the track in New Hampshire.

This was serious. Someone wanted him out of the way. Stumbling along, he tried to reason out where he was. It had been woods track for a while, now it seemed smoother, more like an old woods road.

He thought of the tricks Motorboat had taught him. The trucker had spent hours teaching the boy his own survival skills. How to defend yourself, how to get out of a car when it was underwater, how to escape from a kidnapper. Never talk to strangers, never accept a ride or candy.

None of them helped. With no sight and no sound except his own stumbling steps, and a grunt from his abductor once in a while, he hadn't a clue. Maybe when they got to where they were headed.

Wherever it was, it seemed damp—he could smell it now, a sour smell of swamp and decay, a hint of stagnant water. His captor pushed him forward and he felt himself falling headlong on stones and earth, his mouth in water. He heard the sound of something dragged overhead. He was alone. His hands were tied tightly. He tried to remember all the things he had ever read about escaping, but nothing seemed to fit this situation. He managed to reposition his body and raise his head from the water. It did not seem to be too deep. But his head ached horribly and he could not seem to think.

Enough Peabody, he said to himself, you are in one piss of a fix.

By five o'clock Saturday afternoon Peggy was back at work. Her model's body clad in a red and white striped coverall, the long blonde hair tied back with a red ribbon, she set up the buffet table in the great room, checked ice cubes, mixed punch, and set the coffee urn in place. The water was warming in the lobster pot, and corn, still in its husks, waited on the Monel sink top. The evening meal would be at seven o'clock. A.E. had already signed the three new couples into their respective rooms.

Now, realizing that there was extra food, she picked up the phone to ask Dr. Anna and Lee and Hod if they would like to join the guests that evening.

Dr. Anna demurred. Desultory thoughts of Alexander still haunted her, and she was not quite sure if she wanted to see the lodge again. Sensibility took over. She thanked A.E. an promised to come by at six-thirty. I'm too much alone, thought the older woman, it will do me good to hear some small talk. She rummaged in her closet for a clean skirt and some sort of acceptable blouse for a Saturday night dinner at the lodge. Oh, Alexander, if you were only here.

Lee and Hod stood in the middle of the old tack room at High Meadows and considered the ceiling. Two barn beams ran overhead, and a temporary platform for hay had been built sometime within the past twenty years, but there were several open spaces and they were debating whether it would be worthwhile to put in some sort of wood ceiling.

"It would bring the room together, and why we didn't think of it in the beginning I don't know," Lee said.

"You might say it's because we go at everything backwards." Hod grinned. "Been so busy thinking about getting those bookshelves built and the map table situated and all. I got to admit there's a bit of chaff floating down. Never do for a fellow with hay fever."

"Which you don't have." Lee was amused.

"Nope, missed that. Strictly speaking though, I could have one of the boys fit a tongue-and-groove ceiling up there. Leave the beams exposed. It'll make the room tighter this winter. I'll have to cover things up while he's doing it, should have done it first. But like us, Lee, better late than never. What do you think?"

"I say do it." Lee laughed. "There hasn't been any project around here since I rebuilt Ted and Ellen's cabin."

The phone rang, and Lee listened to A.E.'s voice asking them for dinner.

"Dr. Anna's consented to come. About six-thirty, Lee. We'll start serving at seven. After I get everyone taken care of I can visit with you for a while. I called Enough to ask him if he might be able to come back this evening and help with the dishes, but he doesn't answer. Could you swing around there on your way up? If he's home and could come maybe, you might bring him over."

"Count on us." Lee made motions to Hod, who nodded his head. "Your Saturday night buffets are a tradition. I'll even help with the dishes myself."

At six-twenty that evening they stopped by Motorboat's small neat ranch on the outskirts of Bryant Pond. His car was parked to one side of the driveway but the large truck was gone, and the house appeared to be locked. Peering through the kitchen window, Hod could see a note propped up on the table. There was no sign of Enough.

Hod frowned. "What time did A.E. say he left the lodge."

Lee was also peering through the window. "About three o'clock, she said, and then he was supposed to be going home to do some errands for Motorboat. He ought to be here now. Well, we'll just leave without him. He could have gone off with some other boys for the evening."

"Hum, well maybe we can give him a call from the lodge in another hour. I'll run in and get him for A.E. According to what Motorboat told me, he doesn't mix too much with any other boys. Well—" Hod was thinking out loud.

"You know, you're getting so you're looking for puzzles everywhere. Enough's old enough—" Lee laughed.

"There's one for you—to take care of himself. Come on, I'm hungry for lobster."

Indian Lodge seemed serene in its setting as they drove in the old graveled driveway. A.E. had filled stoneware pots with wildflowers, and a small table with the lodge's punch bowl and cups stood at one end of the long porch. Guests were rocking in the old rocking chairs, and Debby and Chuck Sherman, knowledgeable in the ways of the lodge by grace of their few days stay, were handing around a large tray of canapes. Peggy, in her striped coverall, refilled the punch bowl and A.E. checked the pots in the kitchen.

On this gentle August evening, with just a faint breeze blowing across the lake, with the scent of yellow roses and lilies wafting over the striped lawn, with the view down the lake and across to the mountains, it seemed as though nothing could disturb the serenity of the setting.

Lee and Hod joined the gathering with Dr. Anna close behind them. Dr. Anna took one look at the punch bowl and headed inside for the sideboard in the dining room. A.E., who had seen her face, grinned and followed the short stocky woman into the room.

"The scotch is in the side door down below. I've ice cubes and soda in the kitchen. Help yourself."

"You're a good hostess." Dr. Anna eyeballed the bottle and poured herself a stiff tot. "How are the shakes? I'm going to give you a good going over on Tuesday."

A.E. looked distressed. "Actually, I thought of cancelling. I feel a lot better."

"Don't do that. Just let me give you a once-over, A.E. If you want to spend your golden years fishing on that pond, you'd better take care of yourself now."

"Dr. Anna, did you measure how much scotch you just poured? You're not a good example."

The older woman smiled. Unabashed, she swirled the scotch around, sniffed, and took a sip. "I've drawn down to one a day. I'll expect you on Tuesday."

Neither woman knew the appointment would not be kept. For on Tuesday the whole county would be searching for Enough Peabody. And they would be determined to find him.

Dead or alive.

CHAPTER SIXTEEN

The Shermans had accepted their prolonged stay at Indian Lodge philosophically. But, Saturday morning, after their interview with Dick, they indulged in their first real quarrel.

"I told you." Debby had shown a side Chuck did not know. "I told you I didn't want to come here. Now we won't be back in Boston until Tuesday at the best according to what that hayseed sheriff said. This place is too rustic for me. Even if it was written up by Mr. Wortham. Next time let's go to the Cape."

"If you would just not tell everything we saw we wouldn't be here—it's your fault. What difference does that old man make anyway? Look, Deb, as long as we're in for it, let's make up." They had, and tonight, handing around canapes to the new arrivals, they found they were the center of attention for they had known the murdered man. The new guests decided they had stumbled into a mystery weekend. The ambiance of Indian Lodge and the pond set between the two mountains was all Mr. Wortham had promised. It was turning out to be an adventure.

A.E. and Peggy produced lobsters and corn, rosemary biscuits, vegetable platters, and afterwards strawberry shortcake, Indian pudding and chocolate mousse. Homemade ice cream came out in a hand-cranked freezer, and everyone had a chance to turn the crank. As evening closed in, Dr. Anna leaned back in one of the old rocking chairs and allowed herself a second scotch, and Lee and Hod sat on the steps at her feet and enjoyed their second cup of coffee. A.E. sank down beside them.

"I still can't get Enough on the phone. Peggy said she'd stay and clean up. I don't know what I'd do without that girl."

"She looks like a model," Lee said. "You know, I keep thinking I've seen her someplace but I can't remember where."

"She is a beautiful girl." Dr. Anna sipped her scotch and kept her mouth closed. Of them all, she knew the most about Peggy Canevari.

The moon was rising above the mountain, and A.E. began to feel the tiredness in her bones. It had been a successful evening. The guests scattered to their rooms, and Lee and Hod and Dr. Anna departed. A.E. had thought Motorboat might call, they had a tentative fishing date for Sunday morning early, but if he was in Connecticut that was out. Peggy finished cleaning up in the kitchen and drove away in her small Volkswagen. A.E. walked about turning off lights in the big room and on the porch. Far away in the woods a barred owl called and its mate answered. A shiver ran down A.E.'s spine.

Someone is thinking of me, she thought, wondering if it might be Motorboat, and feeling again the slight shaking of her hands as she turned out the last light. The front door was never locked, but perhaps this was the time to start a new system. She turned the old key, deciding to oil all the locks and check out the cellar doors tomorrow. Tomorrow—after fishing, for even if Motorboat did not join her, she would take the old birchbark canoe out for an hour after sunrise. She climbed the stairs to her room, remembered she had left her notebook in the tower room. She sighed and climbed one more flight to the third story, found the notebook just as she had left it, and turned to snap off the light and leave the room. Her hand on the light switch, she faced the window, admiring the moon's rays on the lake and the dark mass of the mountains. A well of black surrounded the bright moon reflected in the lake.

But there was a diamond of light, a small glow coming from the area of the caves and ledges, a small diamond in a spot where no light should be.

A.E. froze. She rarely came up to the tower room at night. In the daylight she knew that the window looked up to the mountain, but with the summer growth on the trees it was hard to discern the ledges and the cave opening. The few times she had been in the room at night she had never seen a light on the mountainside. Hikers, she thought, then watched the light slowly go on and off. A signal? More likely the person holding the light was passing behind trees. Who would want to be on the mountain at night, much less in the cave area? Who would dare to cross the ledges?

Who indeed?

Chapter Seventeen

The phone was ringing incessantly. A.E. thrust one hand up out from underneath the patchwork quilt and snatched the offender from the hook. Her head ached, and she felt exhausted. She had stayed awake for hours wondering about the light she had seen from the tower room. Sleep had finally come at dawn, and it was now—she opened one bleary eye—it was now only five o'clock. Who—?

There was a noise coming from the phone. Sitting upright and trying to pull her aching body together, she found her hands shaking again as she held the phone to her ear.

"A.E.? What the hell's wrong with you? I thought you'd be up and getting the canoe and bait ready."

"Motorboat? I wasn't sure if you'd come back."

"I didn't. I'm still stuck down here in Connecticut. I won't be back in Maine until tonight. But I figured you'd be going out anyway. Reason I called you is I can't seem to raise Enough. Called him last night. No answer, so I figured he might have stayed over with you. I wanted to tell him I'd be back by six or seven tonight."

A.E.'s hands shook. "Motorboat, he's not here. I called him last night to help with the dishes. Lee and Hod stopped by your place to pick him up. He wasn't there. I don't know where he is."

After a long silence, Motorboat's voice, seemingly controlled, vibrated through the phone.

"A.E., get Dick. Something's wrong. Enough does not go off overnight. He does not do that. Especially with Peggy in your kitchen. Find out who last saw him. I'm on my way up, the tractor will have to wait. It'll take me a bit to get wheels, but I'll be there by noon. Find Dick. Find Hod Cole. Get some men out looking if he doesn't turn up soon. Tell them what I said. And—"

"Yes." She was fully up on her feet now. One hand was reaching for jeans and the sweater thrown over the chair by the bed. "Yes, Motorboat—"

"Forget fishing for the morning. Go down and make some coffee, call Dick, and take care of yourself. There's something going on I don't understand, and if I find out Enough's in trouble, someone will answer to me. I'll be there quick as I can. And A.E.—"

"Yes." The jeans were almost zipped.

"Love you."

A.E. put the phone down gently and pulled the sweater over her head. She hesitated, thinking of Frieda asleep and safe from her own worries, but she dialed Dick and told him of Enough's disappearance.

Frieda murmured in her sleep. Dick had gotten the phone on the first ring. He was used to this, one hand reached out automatically. He listened for a moment, sat up abruptly, and swung his legs down to the floor.

"What time was it when Hod and Lee looked in at Motorboat's house?" he queried.

"Just before six-thirty. We ate at seven, and they came about a half hour before. I didn't think too much of it, so I didn't call back there. I didn't expect to see him until Monday morning."

"I'll go over there right now. He might be home, and the phone's not working, some simple matter. Did you get a number where Motorboat is in Connecticut?"

"No. He said he'd be on his way back within the hour. That means he'll be here by at least noontime."

"Hum. Well, I'll phone you back in a bit. Don't say anything to anyone yet, to Peggy or anyone at the lodge. Not until I get there."

"All right. I'm up now, so I'll make coffee and start some baking. Thanks, Dick."

Indian Pond seemed ominously quiet this morning. The tall redhead sat with her first cup of coffee cradled in her hands, as she did every summer morning, looking across the span of the pond. No mists rose as they had yesterday, no breeze stirred. The light became sharper, early morning pink. The outlines of the shore were bathed in shafts of sunlight. Looking up at the mountain A.E. saw masses of fir and hardwood, darkness giving way to light.

Somewhere, up at the top, there had been a light last night. Or had she dreamed it?

On Motorboat's front porch, Dick, as had Hod and Lee, peeked in the kitchen window. He could see the note propped on the kitchen table. There were still no signs of life. The thought crossed his mind that Enough could be in the house, ill or trapped. He felt about under the doormat and the pots of petunias Motorboat had placed on the porch railing. His hands found the emergency key that every owner always hides somewhere, in this case hung on a small ring under the railing out of sight.

The little ranch house harbored only silence. The note was, as Dick knew, from Motorboat to the boy he rode herd on, the boy who had been rescued from a certain dead-end existence by his maverick uncle. Enough's life had been well programmed by Motorboat, and for him not to come home at the expected time was unusual.

The trooper walked rapidly from room to room, a search that took only moments as the furniture was simple, and it would be difficult to fall behind any of these modern chairs and beds or be hidden in any of the closets with their spartan contents. The cellar was neat, winter's wood for the kitchen stove stood in one corner along with a few neatly stacked boxes and an old bookcase. The large open space of cellar could be seen with one glance and the bulkhead showed empty steps. There were no hiding places. Upstairs again, Dick found the closet with a scuttle to the small open space under the roof, and hiked himself up to look. Just insulation lying over the ceiling, a total open space from end to end. A futile search. Returning to the living room, he picked up the phone. Dial tone, nothing wrong here. He shoved his hat back from his forehead and scratched his head.

Outside again, he opened the garage doors. Here tools, grease guns, everything necessary to a mechanic's life hung in neat rows. No place to hide or be trapped, everything precisely as it should be in a garage. Wherever Enough was, it was not at home base. Dick stood a moment, scratched his head again, and went back to his cruiser to phone the sheriff's office and ask if any new reports had come in. After a negative reply he relayed the information that there could be a missing person. He made a second call to A.E. reporting no sign of Enough at the house and told her he would be at the lodge within an hour.

Then he called Hod Cole.

Sunday morning at High Meadows was a special time for Lee. In all the years she had owned this farm, this was the time she usually spent in the barn with the horses, grooming and cleaning tack. She would take breakfast out to the old long bench in the front of the barn, the quiet bench as Hod called it, and just sit soaking in the aura of the fields and meadows that surrounded the old Cape on the ridge. Now that Hod had come to live here she found herself surprisingly willing to share this time with this unexpected treasure of a man.

Sunday morning breakfasts had become Hod's kitchen time, and this morning he had sauteed tomatoes with eggs and cheese. Two old ironstone dishes held his offering, and thick slices of Anadama bread from the Hungry Hollow shop on Route 26 accompanied the breakfast, along with coffee and juice. Attired in their oldest shirts and jeans, Hod and Lee ate breakfast with their backs to the old barn wall, their plates on their laps and their feet raised up on two wood chunks that had been supporting feet for at least fifty years.

Kate Gordon lay quietly at the barn door, her eyes following the antics of the swallows skimming along the grass, twisting and turning upward like fighter planes heading toward their targets in the crystal clear morning air. Across the paddock the two horses munched grass and stopped with ears at point when deer picked their way carefully through the hardwood stand behind the paddock fence. It was one of those summer mornings when everything seems possible and nothing seems impossible. Pristine. Diamond clear. Totally tangible.

Dick Eggleston's phone call interrupted. Hod answered the ring as he went back in the kitchen to bring out the coffeepot for second cups. The tanned woodsman stood with pot in hand as he listened to Dick's voice. His eyes narrowed.

"I'll join you in about an hour. I suspect Lee'll be with me. Did you ask Peggy, by chance, when she last saw him? A.E. thought he was kind of sweet on her."

The conversation finished, Hod returned to Lee, poured more coffee, and relayed Dick's message.

"I kind of wondered last night when he wasn't home. But I figured he might have gone to a movie or watched TV with friends. Motorboat says he's full of all sorts of dreams, but he's a good boy. No drugs or alcohol there. At least, so far. Maybe we should have gone back after the dinner, Lee."

Lee shook her head. "There's no way to be sure. Where could he be? Do you think this has anything to do with Mr. Fremont's death? Could Enough have seen something?" Her hands gathered plates to take inside. "Now what, Hod?"

"Now we meet up at Indian Lodge. Dick has an alarm out for Enough, and if he doesn't turn up in a few hours there may be a search party. If I don't miss my guess, Dick'll have a few roadblocks. Are you coming with me?"

Lee rinsed plates, neatened the butcher block kitchen counter, and checked the stove. "Yes, but let's take separate cars. Then if you're out on a search for a long while, I can at least get back to feed the horses and walk Kate. Tom and Ellen won't be back until tomorrow night. Hod, who would want to hurt that boy?"

Hod shook his head as he emptied the grounds from the old coffee pot. "Lee, I don't know. I been thinking on all this. Nothing fits in this puzzle. Nothing matches. Mr. Fremont, Robbie, the pony, that old farm with signs of someone driving in there with a horse trailer, but no one there now. We don't even know where that Toyota and the trailer came from, no license plates. Dick has tracers out to several states, but nothing's come in yet; it probably will be next week. And now Enough is missing. Sometimes there's a pattern. But I can't see one here. Do you think Enough might have been doing drugs? Even though Motorboat's sure he didn't."

"No." Lee was emphatic. "Motorboat might look like a good old boy trucker with swinging ways, but he's just the opposite. He's the best thing could ever have happened to Enough. I'd bet he's taught that boy all the right things. I doubt Enough will be tempted with drugs or drink. He's too curious, though. A.E. said he was all excited about finding the body. Maybe that's it. Maybe he saw something he wasn't supposed to see. And A.E. did say, too, that he was sweet on Peggy."

"Peggy Canevari?" Hod's eyes narrowed. "Hum. That blonde in the kitchen, the one in the red striped coverall? The one helping A.E.?"

Lee smiled. "You noticed? Hod, I keep thinking I've seen her before someplace. But I can't think where."

Hod, hauling his low boots out of the old apple box by the door that served as a catchall for outdoor gear, looked up at her. "Well, if Enough was sweet on Peggy, maybe Peggy might know something about where he went. It's worth a question. Just don't say anything until I've had a chance to talk with Dick. You know, I just remembered. I think that girl, or someone who looked like her, used to help at one of those vegetable stands in Oxford. Maybe that's where you saw her. Brought my truck in there one day and used the phone. You don't forget a girl who looks like that. Yessir, I do believe that was Peggy Canevari."

CHAPTER EIGHTEEN

They gathered at the lodge. Dick had put out the word, and from the surrounding towns came woodsmen and businessmen, Maine guides of both sexes, forest wardens, and town sheriffs and deputies from Oxford County. Two state troopers whose families lived in the area came by. Several horseback riders from the Woodstock area drove in, their animals in trailers drawn by pickup trucks of various ages. Three women hikers who had stopped off at a bed and breakfast in Bethel had heard the news that a boy was missing, and they came to volunteer their services.

Over Rowe Hill Road and down the dirt ribbon to Indian Pond to the lodge between the mountains, people gathered. They drew on their Bean boots, lathered themselves with insect repellent, and made ready to search. Enough Peabody was known to many, but Motorboat Jones's name was legend. He had hauled freight from one end of Oxford County to the other, brought food to people who had no money to pay for it, cords of wood for their stoves, sacks of potatoes from his runs into Aroostook County. Fat, sloppy Motorboat, who never graced the interior of a church, had never turned away when someone needed help.

Now it was his turn.

At Indian Lodge, closeted in the tower room, A.E. and Peggy faced each other warily. A.E.'s hands shook. It was nearly eight, and she had been up since five tending kitchen, making muffins, getting ready for what she knew would be a strenuous day. None of the guests were up yet. They were all sleeping in after the lobster feed the night before, so A.E. had had time for her morning cup of coffee on the steps facing the pond, but this morning there had been a sense of doom hanging over the mountains, and when Peggy drove in at eight sharp, A.E. was waiting for her.

"Peggy, we need to talk." The lodge owner moved rapidly along the hallway and up the staircase with the younger woman following behind her. "When did you last see Enough?"

Peggy hesitated. She had heard the news this morning at the doughnut shop, when she had stopped to buy coffee, but it had only been a snatch of conversation that a boy was missing from Indian Lodge and that he was Motorboat Jones's ward. Driving up the valley she had thought of what she would say, but she had not expected to be attacked so fast. For a moment she drew back, contemplating just what she could say to this obviously distraught woman.

"He left at three when I took my two hours off. That's the last I saw of him. How should I know anyway?"

A.E. hesitated. She was not sure of her ground.

Maybe this should be left to Dick. But— "I know he followed you sometimes. You told me that yourself. I just wondered if he did yesterday. If you might have seen him on the path. I know you go up on the mountain. Peggy, I've never asked you anything. Your life is your own. But if you know anything, you must say. He's been missing all night. It just isn't like Enough. Motorboat's on his way up from Connecticut, and Dick is gathering a search party. People will headquarter here. No one saw Enough along Rowe Hill Road. Nobody saw him bicycle through town. So I just thought he might have followed you —"

"Well, he did. At least I think he did. I'll be glad to tell Dick Eggleston that. I don't know what happened to him. I didn't see him after about five minutes. I just drew back in the bushes and let him pass by. He was a nuisance, A.E. I don't wish him any harm, but he was a nuisance."

"Was?" A.E.'s voice was cold. "Where were you going anyway?"

"I don't have to tell you that." Peggy was angry. The blonde curls tossed. She shrugged her shoulders. "It's really none of your business, is it?"

"I know it isn't, but—"

"Then leave it alone. You don't really want to know."

"Peggy, I don't want to know who you see. But I am concerned about Enough. If there's any chance you have some information—"

"I haven't. May I go down now? They'll all be awake soon."

A.E. felt helpless. Part of her, the redhaired, Irish-tempered part, longed to shake Peggy Canevari out of her cold complacency, the other part drew back from any involvement. No, she really did not want to know. Let Dick take care of it. Things would be better that way.

The new arrivals were stirring, the Shermans already in the dining room. A.E. greeted them. "Peggy will be out with coffee in a moment. We have blueberry coffee cake this morning. And, by the way, there will be a gathering of people on the porch. We are headquarters for a search. The boy who mows lawns and helps us here seems to be missing. You might want to tell the other guests that when they come down."

Somehow the Shermans seemed like old friends. They'd been in on Mr.

Fremont's death and they'd been helpful last evening with the guests. She felt a new warmth toward them.

"Do you think all this confusion will put the guests off?" She felt anxious as she asked the question.

"I think it's exciting. Sort of like a mystery weekend. Mr. Wortham said to expect the unexpected here. May we watch the searchers start?" Debby was excited.

"I'm sure they won't mind. Actually we may need more help. I may have to feed some of these people."

"When did he disappear?" Debby was fascinated. Today she wore a magenta pullover with walking shorts. A magenta bandanna covered the back of her dark blonde hair. Large golden hoops swung from her ears and her face was carefully made up with sunscreen. "I saw him yesterday on the porch steps."

"When?" A.E. carefully set the pewter coffeepot on the serving tray at the side of the room.

"Around three o'clock. I was down by the pond in a deck chair, and I came back up to get a book. I remember I spoke to him, and he answered. He seemed to be peeking around the big log porch column."

Watching for Peggy, thought A.E. Dick has to hear this. Cars sounded on the driveway, and A.E. knew the police had arrived. She excused herself and went through the swinging doors into the kitchen to find Peggy doing eggs and arranging the blueberry coffee cake on a tray. Giant raspberries and blueberries were mixed in a high, footed compote of Portland glass, and small glasses of pineapple juice were ready for serving. Dick came through the outside door just as A.E. picked up the compote and the small serving dishes.

"Can I count on you for coffee? We're going to have a crowd. The alarm is out, and you know how many friends of Motorboat's will drop everything to help. Have you heard any more from him?"

"Just that one call. He must be on his way. There'll be plenty of coffee. Muffins, too. And if it goes on all day, I think we can put out some sort of sandwich tray for them. Dick—"

She motioned him into the dining room. He waited by the door as she served the Shermans, assured them the rest of their breakfast was on its way, and then waved Dick down the hall to the phone area by the bathroom under the stairs.

"Peggy saw him last. She admitted he was following her yesterday afternoon. You may be able to get more information out of her, I just seem to rub her the wrong way. Dick, I'm really worried."

"I am too. This isn't like him, and I'm mounting a search of the whole mountainside. A.E., what about Robbie?"

"Robbie?"

"He knows that mountain and the swamp better than anyone. When you're done here with breakfast, maybe you'll ride over with one of my deputies to bring him over. He won't be scared if you go along with the deputy. And you know his mind. He'll come for you."

"Of course. Robbie. Dick, you know he's different. I told you that. He may have some thoughts as to where Enough is—"

"You mean that physic powers bit. He can read minds. You really believe that."

"I know he can sometimes. It's worth a try. I'll ask him where Enough might be. Perhaps he can think it through and give us a clue. Maybe Enough's fallen or been trapped in a slash pile. Maybe he's badly hurt."

"Maybe. But if he can shout, we'll hear him. If he's alive and on the mountain, we ought to find him. If he's in the swamp, well that's another story. He must be somewhere around this mountain area. No one saw him pedal down Rowe Hill Road and no one saw him in Bryant Pond or Locke Mills."

Dick paused as the sound of the guests descending the stairs reached his ears. Together, he and A.E. escaped to the porch, Dick putting his arm around the tall redhaired woman and patting her shoulder.

"It will come out all right. I don't believe any real harm has come to him. I think he's just caught someplace, not able to call out. We'll find him."

"Go on now, with your searchers. You must be having a bad patch yourself right now. How is Frieda?"

The trooper shook his head. "She still feels uncomfortable. Dr. Anna came by and that helped a little, just having her there, but things aren't ever going to be the same until the baby's born. Frieda is so afraid of what might happen. I don't know how to help her."

"I'll go over tomorrow when I'm in town. I'm remiss, I haven't seen her in two weeks. I'm so sorry, Dick, this must be difficult for you both."

The trooper sighed and turned to greet a tall, gangly horseman arriving with a beat up old trailer that looked more like a fish house than a horse carrier. The man raised one hand in silent greeting to the trooper and proceeded around the back to unload a skittish gray gelding with crooked legs and a sway back.

"Got the word, Dick. Anytime Motorboat Jones needs help, I'm there. Which way we heading?"

"It'll be a while yet. I have to see how many searchers we have. There's coffee up here on the corner of the porch. At least, there will be pretty quick."

Two men came out of the kitchen, lugging a set up table followed by a woman dressed in old jeans with a blue tee shirt labeled DON'T GIVE ME ANY CRAP.

"I wasn't planning to," Dick murmured, almost in awe at this outfit placidly and expertly setting up the food table, running wires to a porch outlet to connect the big coffee urn, and setting out platters of muffins Peggy had taken from the freezer on A.E.'s instructions. Within minutes all was in order. Two cocker spaniels that had arrived with a couple from Norway expressed hope, but their owners put them firmly back in the car.

"You just tell us where you want things, Mz. Gibbons." A woman in a silver-shot long-sleeved shirtwaist and faded denim skirt poured coffee from a thermos Peggy had brought out earlier while they waited for the coffee to be made.

"Motorboat brought us wood one winter when my man was laid off from the dowel factory. That was one bad winter, and he helped us. Wouldn't take a cent, just said to pass it on. Well, maybe we can help find his boy now." She measured coffee expertly into the fifty-cup pot and plugged it into the extension cord. " Looks like it might blow up. Mind if we put this outfit inside if it rains? "

" Anyplace you want." A.E. extended a hand. "I'm glad you're here. Motorboat is a good friend of mine too."

The woman smiled and shook hands. "I'm Billie Trafton. There's been Traftons up and down this valley as long as it's been here, I guess. I'm pleased to know you. I heard about you helping Robbie Moulton. You and that real estate lady. Guess we all help each other when the time comes. Don't you worry, I'll take care of people out here. I know you have lodge guests."

A.E. felt relief. Most of the people rolling in she knew by sight or reputation. And Lee and Hod would be here soon. The lodge routine could go on, with people like Billie Trafton taking care of the searchers.

I forgot, thought A.E. I forgot. Everything comes full circle. Maine people pull together. And this is Motorboat's circle.

Coming around.

Within an hour Dick planned to have searchers fanning out, up the trails, up the mountainside, in the swamp area.

An old woman who rocked regularly on her porch fronting on Rowe Hill Road reported no sign of Enough cycling downward around three o'clock, as he would have been expected to do on a Saturday afternoon. His bicycle was discovered parked behind one of the pine trees on the edge of the lawn, almost as though Enough had put it there purposely in case he needed to travel one of the lower trails. His whereabouts were still a mystery.

Dick, before starting the searchers in different directions, talked with Peggy. In a few words she told him exactly the same story she had told A.E. that morning.

"Do you think he might have caught on and followed you anyway? Just where did you go?" Dick watched the blue eyes.

"No, I lost him. I just walked up to the old house site halfway up the mountain. I sat there for about an hour, took a nap. It's good to get away from the lodge, especially when A.E.'s so pressured about the guests coming in and she fusses about the food. Then I walked back down. I have to get away sometimes. Don't you know?" She eyed Dick thoughtfully.

Better to tell a half truth, my girl. Never lie, just tell part of the truth. Peggy had learned that early on.

"You didn't see anyone else? You didn't go to meet anyone?" Dick watched the blue eyes flicker, avoid his gaze. They came back to meet his stare with a look that made the kitchen seem cold even on this August morning.

"I told you." Peggy's voice was sharp. "No one."

"Do you think he knew the trails well?" Dick knew if he kept talking some overlooked fact might emerge. "Would you think he might have gotten lost? Are there any slash piles up there?"

"Probably." Peggy saw a new direction. " Yes, I'd say that's possible. Those trails wind all over the mountain. He could have gotten lost. Or caught in a slash pile and hurt. Easily."

Dick shook his head and turned away. "You're here all day today, aren't you?"

"Just until after lunch. I'm off Sunday afternoons."

"Well, be where I can find you. I might need to talk with you again."

Peggy nodded, expertly setting out eggs for the guests' omelets and adding seasoning to the mixture. "I'll be right here."

Dick departed to rejoin the ladies on the porch.

Peggy moved quickly through the kitchen, into the hallway to the phone beside the bathroom door. She took the receiver from its hook and dialed a number.

"I told you never to call here."

"Enough didn't go home last night. There's a big search party out for him. Do you know anything about this? Do you know where he is?"

The answering voice was soothing, kindly. "No, I didn't see anyone when I came down off the mountain. He's probably just gone off with some friends. They'll find him. Don't call here again, though. I'll get in touch with you. Not to worry."

Peggy hung up, still uneasy and unconvinced.

CHAPTER NINETEEN

At eleven o'clock on this Sunday morning in August there was a stillness in the air, a pause as if the elements were deciding whether the day would be clear or cloudy, windy or calm, their wishes visited upon mere mortals below. Dick's eyes searched the sky, then turned to scan the surface of Indian Pond. Could Enough lie beneath the water?

They will search the mountain first, then deal with the pond, the one spot no one even wants to consider. Besides, Enough is a good swimmer. So they will search the mountain trails and the swamp—those areas alone will take two or three days. Combing a mountainside is different from flat or swamp land. Uphill going is rough, and the numerous trails leading nowhere are disheartening. Dick considered all this as, all about him, men and women waited to start.

"Sweep in lines, four or five of you in a group—try to cover every piece of ground. Look at any old house cellars, old wells, every slash heap you see. He may have fallen and be trapped somewhere. Listen for sounds every once in a while, and I'll fire a signal if we find anything. Two shots, everyone will know we've found him. One shot, I'm calling you back in to the lodge. Watch out for each other, there are rocks near the top. I'll appoint one group just to do the cave and ledge area."

Dick's thoughts turned to kindergarten instruction. "Help each other."

Slim, the tall deputy, had motioned people to sign before they started out. This had been Hod's idea, spoken in sotto voice to Dick when the older man arrived, moccasins on his feet and his old, worn woods clothing adorning his person. Hod had done this before. He had found two lost children who had strayed away from a camping area, and he knew that searchers themselves could become turned around in the woods and be a hindrance to the search rather than an asset. A log book let you know who was out there when nightfall came, and unless Hod was far wrong, his instincts told him this could be a long search. He, like Dick, had thoughts of the pond. He hoped it wouldn't come to that in the end.

On the porch of the lodge the guests watched, fascinated by the show of force from the natives, the camaraderie, the preparations of men and women and horses and the unspoken feeling of purpose. Rather than putting the guests off, as A.E. had feared, the search preparations for the missing boy seemed to intrigue them. Perhaps they wished that their urban neighbors might care enough to look for them were they lost among the caverns of the cities.

There was little conversation as the guests watched the men and women start out on their sweep of the mountain and the swamp.

Lee helped Peggy and A.E. in the kitchen. A.E. took frozen food from the freezer. Peggy sliced bread and created sandwiches to wrap in foil for later in the day.

"Have you heard any more from Motorboat?" Lee's hands dealt with paper cups and plastic spoons, while her mind thought of Enough, somewhere on the face of the earth, but where?

"No. He should be here by noon. He's a strange man, Lee. He looks so big and sloppy, but he's taught that boy well. I know this has nothing to do with alcohol or drugs. And Enough wouldn't want to run away. Why should he? He worships Motorboat. I keep wondering if there are any animals on the mountain that might have bothered him? Coyotes shouldn't attack a person, black bears don't usually unless you bother their cubs, we don't have panthers or mountain lions anymore. And I don't believe a bobcat would hurt a person. For all he's a dreamer, Enough is no fool. I keep thinking he may have fallen someplace."

"I'm sure that's it." Peggy joined in. "I'll bet he's trapped somewhere, maybe twisted his ankle and can't walk."

"Then why doesn't he call out?" A.E. looked at the younger woman.

"They'll find him, I know they will." Peggy seemed certain.

Lee listened to the exchange between the two women, then walked out on the porch to join the remaining deputy. Within a few minutes she returned to the kitchen.

"A.E., do you want to drive over to Robbie's? The deputy will take us over. We're supposed to ask Robbie if he has any feeling for where Enough might be, on or off the mountain."

"Dick did mention that, although he's a nonbeliever in Robbie's powers. It's worth a try. Yes, I'll go."

Half an hour later, Lee and A.E., with Slim at their side, sat on the wooden bench by Robbie's camp. The little man, his hands working on the rim of a gathering basket, wound the ash splints with care as he stared straight ahead.

"Dark, smells like damp. Stones someplace. A ring of stones." He sat motionless, eyes blank, hands still. "Stones."

A.E.'s voice was low. "Where, Robbie? Can you see where?"

Eyes closed, Robbie hummed a half-forgotten tune his mother had used when she looked into the mountain. She could see the stands of black ash, the ginseng plants beneath the pines, the betony for her healing teas. She could tell when a person was marked for death, her eyes searching a face—

"Won't make old bones." He remembered her voice as she sat with the baskets between her knees, her cracked fingers weaving beauty. "Won't make old bones."

Now Robbie looked, using her eyes, her teaching. It made him nervous, only because A.E. and Lee asked would he try to help find the boy. He was not a nice boy anyway—he had teased Robbie several times, calling him Swamper and laughing at him when he worked with the bees. Never mind. A.E. had asked and he would try. He strained to see the mountain and the swamp. To see what held the boy.

"Just stones. Can't see no more. Just stones. But a deep place. Someone else nearby." He shook his head and drew back, folded within himself, hunted rather than the hunter.

"No more."

A.E. patted his shoulder. "It's all right, Robbie. That could help. Maybe later you can try again. I know it takes a lot out of you."

As Lee moved off to one side, giving A.E. and Robbie a moment together, Slim joined her.

"Do you really believe that, Ms. Heaward? That he has psychic powers?"

"I don't know. I guess I think he can read minds. I know his mother had a reputation for second sight. Maybe he's inherited her gift. He certainly hasn't been exposed to many people, although he went as far as the eighth grade. She was his whole world. Maybe I do believe he can see into the mountain. Anyway, it's worth a try."

"Stones, he said. Half the damn mountain is stone. That boy could be anyplace. And he said deep. Could be the bottom of the lake."

She shuddered. "Please not."

They did not bring Robbie back to the lodge with them.

Suspicious as he was of people, he was more help at his own camp, on his own turf. A second visit, a second reaching into the mountain, might release more information. For now, the word *stones* was all they had to go on. Somewhere, Enough was near stones.

Hod searched alone. He could see the line of people, stretching out across part of the mountain, directly across from the lodge. This was the first wave, going in the same direction Peggy had followed with Enough on her trail. The man with the crooked-legged gray gelding took the path upward to the caves, stopping now and then to look down at the bushes along the trail. Up on a horse, it's a different view. You see things you miss on level ground. The man's old trail rider eyes looked for clues—a piece of cloth, blood, signs of a scuffle. Anything.

Enough was defeated. For a long while he had lain unconscious, for how long he did not know, but he had finally surfaced with an aching head and a dampness in his bones. He tried to loosen his hands but he had no strength. The gag bound round his mouth was hindering his breathing. He remembered Motorboat's instructions on how to get out of bonds, find something sharp and keep rubbing against it—but there was nothing sharp within reach. It was cold and wet and hard, stone hard under him and behind him. He could hardly move his body, and his jeans were soiled and wet from his own terror as well as from the surroundings. He was scared.

He tried to think of Motorboat's survival course. 'If you're in a bad pickle you have to think your way out. Nobody but you to do it.'

That was the day they'd discussed being underwater in a car. "Keep your head, no matter how scared you are." Motorboat's words came back. "Nobody but you to do it."

For the first time, Enough felt he might have a chance. Maybe he could find a way out. Think, boy, think. He remembered Motorboat's face, round and red-cheeked, bending over a flat tire, replacing spark plugs, rebuilding motors.

Think, boy, think. But they had never discussed the possibility of attempted murder.

Motorboat's mind followed the same pattern. All the way up the turnpike from Connecticut he had thought of Enough. Wherever you are, boy, if you're still alive, I'm coming. People's minds follow the same route in time of distress, signaling to their families, their loved ones the message to hang on. Wait until I'm there to die, wait until I'm there to help you, wait until I'm at your side. Then it will be all right, then we can do whatever must be done together. Motorboat's mind reached out to the boy deep within the old stone cistern.

Hang on, Enough, I'm coming.

CHAPTER TWENTY

Motorboat arrived near noon. At the same time another car drove in beside him; Walter Desmond had heard the news on the morning radio and had come over from the cottage across the pond to see if he could help. Carol and the children were still in Massachusetts, and Walter, after his usual run, spent most of the morning in his garden. Coming in for a cup of coffee, he had turned on the local station.

About the same time, Bill Bannerman had turned on his battery radio. He sat methodically drinking his morning coffee laced with Jack Daniels, then rose and fried himself two pieces of stout bacon along with three eggs. He placed his dishes in the enamel pan in the old tin sink, and picked up his stout walking staff. He closed and locked the cabin door, placed the key on a nail driven in the trunk of a nearby maple tree, and set out toward Indian Lodge.

Old Bill had a lot of thinking to do. He did it best while he walked. Alexander's death puzzled him, and he had come to the conclusion that Alexander had found something in or near the caves that the murderer couldn't allow to be seen. The two men had become close during their summers together, close enough for Bill to know Alexander was interested in Dr. Anna. Alexander had intimated it might become more than friendship this summer.

"Think me a bit of an old fool, Bill?" Alexander had needed to take counsel with his companion.

"No, I hear she drinks like a lady. She'd be lucky to get you, Alexander. I just don't want her interfering with our digging."

Alexander had chuckled. "No fear of that. I don't think she'd want to have a man under her feet all day long. I'd be just as free to come and go as I am now." And he had smiled at the possibility of marrying Dr. Anna.

Old Bill, picking his way up the trail, passing the Confluence and meeting three men from the search party, kept thinking of his friend. What had he seen? What had he found? Had he recognized someone up here in Maine, someone from the past who didn't want to be recognized? Old Bill's mind considered all possibilities. He had probably found something, something he was taking back to the lodge when he was killed. Why else would he be going back on a day he was supposed to be digging?

Bill was closer to the lodge now, out of the woods and nearing the building. He wanted to talk with Dick Eggleston, perhaps help with the search. His legs were still strong, although he avoided steep slopes. Maybe he'd be better in the swamp or on one of the lower trails. Dick would find a place to use him. And he knew A.E. would be feeding the searchers. He looked forward to some of her cooking.

Funny how women are, he thought, as he strode along. First thing they think of in an emergency is setting up a coffee urn and getting out some food. Fire or flood, they'd set up and serve the workers. A good thing. Bill smiled, one of his rare smiles. Maybe Dr. Anna would be there. The thought brought him a little closer to his old friend.

While Bill was coming toward them across the meadow, Dick was briefing Motorboat and Walter Desmond on the areas to search. Motorboat said little, listened intently while Dick brought him up to date, and accepted coffee from A.E., who leaned forward and kissed him on the cheek. Another time there would have been a snide remark. Today it meant much to both of them, and his arm encircled her waist for a second, before he dropped it and turned back to Dick Eggleston.

"Where is Hod?"

"He said he'd check the trails on the edge of the swamp. Over by the Indian monument. We have a group sweeping halfway up, a couple of riders near the cave trails, and a group over toward the edge of the pond. People are supposed to shout out every so often in case he's trapped. He might hear and answer. Look, these are the areas we're trying to cover."

He traced a grid on a topographical map spread out on the table.

"I'll take this path along the pond." The trucker sighed. "You planning on a drag of the pond, Dick, if we don't find him on the mountain?"

The trooper looked at Motorboat's tired face, saw the effort the sentence had cost him, and merely nodded. They both knew that was the last resort and one they didn't want to face. They also both knew they would face it when the time came.

Walter leaned over the map. "Look, maybe I can help Hod in this area. There are so many old trails around the swamp. You know, Robbie might be able to help there."

"We've already contacted him." Lee joined the conversation. "I think he's going to stay at his camp, not come over here. He's still under suspicion, and he doesn't want to talk with anyone. He's pretty upset."

"I can appreciate that." The banker smiled at A.E. as she stood alongside Motorboat. "That family always was a little different. I remember Robbie in school—third grade I think it was. He never mixed with anyone."

"Robbie would never harm anyone." Motorboat's statement was flat out.

"I've known people you'd never think would steal, either." Walter faced the trucker. "You never really know what people are capable of doing."

Dick brought them back from what seemed the beginning of an argument with instructions on keeping in touch with the rest of the searchers. Motorboat and Walter, an unlikely pair, started along the trail hugging the pond. The banker followed the fat man for a short distance, then branched off by himself on a lower trail along the edge of the swamp.

Hod searched alone. His mind ticked off all possible places Enough could be trapped, all the reasons Mr. Fremont might have been killed, and all the reasons why the Toyota and the horse trailer, without license plates, were hidden back in at the old farm. He had intended to ask Dick if any new information had come in since yesterday. It would take a while for out-of-state replies to Dick's inquiries. There was nothing that bound these three mysteries together. And yet, and yet, maybe there was. Hod could almost smell the connection.

Whatever the clues were, the puzzle would finally be solved. Today it was important to find Enough Peabody.

Ten minutes later, Hod did find a body. But it wasn't the lost boy. It was the man on the other end of the foot under the cache of stones by the Indian monument. The man with an Ace bandage on his ankle. The man who obviously was not coming back to the old farm to claim his gear and his horse trailer. The man who connected all three mysteries.

Chapter Twenty-One

Hod hunkered down alongside the stone cache. He brushed aside the late summer goldenrod and the purple fall asters that edged the pathway and the burial cache. His eyes scanned the ground, looking for signs of life, signs made by whoever had brought this body here for burial. Hod's woodsman's eyes saw every broken twig, every place a footprint might have been made, every area that could leave a clue. Yet there seemed to be few clues. If the body had been dragged here, some of the small bushes encroaching on the edge of the narrow path should have be broken.

Nothing. But looking upward, above what would have been waist high for a man carrying a body, up above that line, there were a few broken twigs. One small swamp oak looked as though something might have broken off the top. Something five feet off the ground. And off to the left of the path, just on the edge, almost underneath a small beaten-down bush, was a hoofprint.

A horse. The body came in on a horse. Or alive—maybe the person came in on a horse. Hod realized he did not know whether this was man or woman. It looked, what he could see of it, like a man's foot. A man's foot with the ankle bound with an Ace bandage.

A light mist was beginning to fall, and Hod felt a sadness. He had to know. It could be Enough beneath that pile of stones. No one had said anything about his ankle being injured, but it was for Enough they were searching. All the rules said to get help, but Hod had to know. Very carefully he removed stones from where the upper end of the body should be and exposed the head, positioned sideways, with the back of the skull damaged. Dried blood stained and the skin, and deterioration had set in. Hod's lips set in a tight line. Someone had again committed murder.

But it was not , thank the Lord, Enough. It was no one Hod had ever seen. He knew who it was, who it had to be. The man who had left his food and clothing at the old farm. The man who had brought a horse trailer to Maine. And the man that had either ridden or been carried to his death on a horse.

Howard. Hod whispered the name under his breath. Howard. What else did Robbie Moulton know?

The mist was thicker now, a gentle rain. Clouds were pressing in, the light was fading even at this early hour, and it was becoming, as they said in the old days, a loury day. Hod debated. Should he put the stones back over the face? If he didn't, and it rained hard, some of the blood and evidence might be removed. Best to put them back. As his hand reached out for the first stone he heard the sound of footsteps.

Hod was a tracker. His nickname long before he had ever met Lee Heaward had been "Old Poacher." He drew back into the brush to one side of the cache, hidden from view. His thoughts raced. Had he made any sounds someone might have heard? Had he indicated his location? There'd been no reason to be quiet. He had felt quite alone there, hunkering down by the stone cache surrounded by the wild grasses and flowers of the swamp. There was no reason not to make himself known.

And yet he crouched quietly, hardly breathing, his eyes steely, narrowed in anticipation.

Walter Desmond walked into view, looking to either side and then down at the stone cache. "My God, my God, how did this happen?" He looked down at the exposed face. He paled and leaned against the monument for support. The old granite marker had once been surrounded by a fence, but that was long gone and now, almost hidden by brush and tangled berry vines, only this side of the monument facing the pile of stones could still be reached. The banker's hand covered his eyes and he seemed to be having trouble breathing.

Hod parted the bushes. "Take a deep breath. It'll help. I had the same reaction."

"My God. Where did you come from?" Walter was completely unstrung.

"I found him about ten minutes ago. Heard you coming down the path and didn't know who it was. Look, put your head down. You look as though you might faint." Hod grinned to himself. These bankers weren't made of tough stuff.

"It's the shock." Walter shook his head and wiped his face with a blue bandanna he took from the rear pocket of his jeans. "What do you think happened?"

"Well, he didn't bury himself. Looks like somebody goes around bashing people on the back of the head. I was looking for Enough along the swamp area. Thought I remembered—"

Walter had given up and was retching on one side of the path. Wiping his face again, he seemed more composed.

"I feel better now. I'll stay here if you want to go back and get Dick. I started out with Motorboat, then branched off on this old trail. I feel like I better sit down. Here." Walter followed his own advice and sat on a fallen log.

Hod stood thinking, his eyes scanning the area, his mind considering possibilities. Should he go back, or should he send Walter back? Maybe they both should go. What was it that kept coming to his mind, elusive, not to be pinned down. Something he should remember. Something important.

"We'll both go back. This fellow's not going anywhere. It's only a short walk back to the main branch of the trail, and Dick's probably at the lodge. Everyone'll be coming back in to get rain gear if this keeps up. Let's go back together." Hod's voice was decisive.

Back at the lodge the rain was increasing. The women had repositioned the food table in the great room. Someone had started the stone fireplace. lodge guests and searchers alike were warming their bodies. August can be chill, and the searchers, defeated for today, felt a sense of depression for a job not finished. The thought of a boy, somewhere in the forests or the pond, dead, perhaps never to be found, filled the minds of several people. By twos and threes they straggled in, wringing water from their jeans, pulling on warmer clothing stored in cars and trucks, sipping coffee. A laconic gathering.

The women at the table knew the signs. They offered food and warmth. They spoke softly, listened, made small comments. They had chattered like squirrels this morning, almost enjoying the beginning of the search, but now they were in a somber mood, knowing the chances of finding the boy alive were slimmer. The rain increased, and Dick looked for the faces of Motorboat and Hod and Walter Desmond.

The three men met at the branch of the trail. Their feet moved faster now they were closer to the lodge. Hod told Motorboat of the stone cache, and both men knew they would be returning to it, rain or not, as soon as they reported to Dick. Walter, who jogged regularly, had no trouble keeping up with Hod, but Motorboat was puffing as they mounted the steps of Indian Lodge.

A.E., looking out the old floor-length windows into the now driving rain, saw them coming. Dick, still logging people in, found a strange relief at the sight of Hod. He turned toward the woodsman, knowing something had happened.

"Dick, we found a body. No, A.E., it's not Enough."

The woman drew in her breath. Hod's eyes searched for Lee.

"Can't tell for sure, but looks like it might be the man who came in to the farm. Ankle's bandaged. Lee—"

She had appeared from the kitchen, bearing another tray of Peggy's sandwiches in one hand and slices of applesauce cake on a dish in the other. iYou're soaking wet."

"No matter. There's an extra shirt and pants out in the truck. Lee, remember the trailer you followed? Can you recall what the man looked like when you passed him?"

Lee shook her head. "Not really. Is it important?"

Hod nodded as he sipped hot coffee. "Might be that trailer out at the old farm could be the one you saw. Might be that body in the stone cache could be the man driving the trailer. Might be—"

Lee interrupted suddenly. "Hod, you said stone. The stone cache?"

"By the Indian monument. The body's buried underneath the stone cache by the monument."

"Stones. Hod, that was the word Robbie used. Stones. That we would find Enough near stones." Her voice trembled.

Hod, his mind suddenly alert in his tired, wet body, stood still. "Stones. Thank you, Lee. Now I know what I've been trying to remember. I think I might know where Enough could be." He turned toward Motorboat, who stood dripping water on the old pine floor.

"I think I know where he is. Let's haul freight, Motorboat. He may still be alive."

CHAPTER TWENTY-TWO

Outside, Dick fired one shot to call in the remaining searchers. The rain had intensified now, beating fiercely on the lawn and gardens around the lodge. Wind swayed the treetops of the hardwood stand and the mountainside. The exposed rock and ledges would begin to be slick, and there was no sense in having anyone hurt, wherever Enough was. By now it was darkening although it was only four in the afternoon. They could start again on Monday.

Dick, after firing the signal, stood in the driving rain talking with Slim. They considered Hod's discovery. Inside, Lee insisted Hod exchange his wet clothing for dry, and while he changed in the downstairs bathroom under the stairs, Motorboat stripped down out in his pickup. He never traveled without a change. All his vehicles had brown paper bags with clean old clothing in them for the times he had to change tires on a wet highway or help someone out of a roadside ditch.

Motorboat was tired, more tired than he cared to admit to himself. Folds of flesh made squeezing into his dry jeans an effort, and he decided an exercise program had to be started soon to make up for the days of driving back and forth across the country. Exercise, that was it, more time to go fishing with A.E., more time to start a jogging program like that lean banker followed. More of something, he thought, as he grunted leaning over to pull on dry socks.

"Hod's ready," Lee called from the porch. "Walter's going too."

Walter Desmond always came prepared, probably a throwback to his Scout days. He was warm now in a dry wool sweater and jeans under lightweight rain gear. He had changed quickly ahead of the other two men, and he stood on the porch sipping coffee and listening to Dick thank the searchers and give them details for Monday.

"We'll start as soon as we can if this rain stops. Anyone who can come will be appreciated. I know some of you can't come."

He shook hands with the man who owned the crooked-leg gelding, and asked if he'd heard of any stray horses. The man shook his head, said he'd inquire around, and then hurried to load his own skittish mount in his fish house trailer. After considerable coaxing and swearing and the use of an old burlap bag over his head, the gelding consented to loading, and they were off and away up the driveway toward Rowe Hill Road.

Lee, watching the entire operation in silence, suddenly turned to Dick. "He loaded on the left-hand side."

"I should hope so." Dick wondered if Lee was as tired as he felt.

"Well, that trailer I followed up from Gray a couple of weeks ago had a horse loaded on the right. I remember now I thought someone didn't know much about horses. But the trailer did have a Massachusetts plate. Did you send an inquiry to Massachusetts?"

"I put an inquiry into a central listing—it should go out to all New England states. Sometimes it takes a while to get back. But I'll double-check that. Hod, you ready to go back out in this rain?" The woodsman had joined them.

"Yup. I think I know where Enough might be. Motorboat is going with us. We won't be too long with three of us to search. There's several old cellar holes near that monument. According to my map there was a settlement there once on the edge of the swamp. Those old houses had cisterns with stone linings. Shallow wells, too, with stone walls. Could be he's stumbled into one of them, hurt himself, and can't get out. I want to look before it gets dark. And it's close on already with this rain." His eyes scanned the sky.

"Wouldn't he call out?" Peggy stood on the porch looking at the men.

"Not if he was unconscious. I'll feel better if I just check that area once more. I should have thought of it before." Hod handed his cup to Lee and pulled on an old wool hat. "Let's go."

Walter Desmond fell in behind Hod and Motorboat. "If we split up, we could cover more ground. I'm good for another hour at least. Hod, if you and Motorboat take one area I'll try another. I know that ground pretty well myself. I take those trails sometimes when I'm on my morning runs. I do believe I know where those old house sites are, on the low edge of the swamp."

Motorboat felt better. He was warm and dry now and there were companions to help in the search. Three men were together looking for the boy. The trucker had begun to think Enough was in the pond, lying on the bottom against rocks and sand, gone forever. But now there was hope and checking the old house sites delayed facing the dragging of the pond.

"I'm all set." He zipped up his old windbreaker, bent his head against the wind, and moved forward.

"Remember, Robbie said stones," Lee called after Hod. "And be careful, will you? He said there was danger, too. Be careful."

Hod turned and retraced his steps. He bent down to her, touching her cheek with his hand. "I mind exactly what he said. Which is why I want to check those sites. There are three of us, Lee. We won't be long. I should have thought of it when I was out there. Stop worrying, now. Something's bothering you, isn't it?"

Lee nodded, grateful he understood. "I don't know what it is. But Robbie said danger. So, please, I don't want anything to happen to you."

Dick, still talking with the departing searchers, waved the three men on their way. He checked his car radio for any late information from out of state and turned to reenter the lodge. Peggy and A.E. were cleaning up the kitchen while the new lodge guests stood about in the great room admiring the roaring fire in the large stone fireplace. Soon bridge and mahjong would take their full attention as had the morning's search for the lost boy. Their lives had been momentarily interrupted, their vacations enlivened by the activity, something to talk about back in the city. Cocktail talk. Unlike the people who had climbed the mountainside, stumbling over slash piles and rock ledges, their worlds far apart.

Lee, bundling paper cups in a garbage bag, was glad she had thought of the flashlights. Hod always wore a small one, finger size, hung about his neck on a heavy silver chain that she had given him for their first-year anniversary. The chain hung low, inside his shirt, and could not be noticed, the light a slim pencil that still spread a wide enough beam to light the way on a path in unexpected darkness. Motorboat always kept a light in his truck, and Lee had found an extra one in the kitchen for Walter. Looking into a well might require light.

Hod smiled inwardly, thinking how often their thoughts meshed without verbal communication. Striding forward, head down in the driving rain, he thought of Robbie. Stones. Of course. Why hadn't he thought of it before?

The three men separated where the trail branched and entered the swamp area. Hod found the first site, a low area indicating where there might have been a building, but there was no well or cistern. Motorboat's sharp eyes found another possibility, but still nothing—the ground was uneven and soggy on the swamp's edge, but there were no holes where a boy might be trapped. Walter found an actual stone opening within fifty feet of the monument. The men were within shouting distance of one another, and their voices boomed through the rain and the increasing wind.

"Any luck?" Motorboat called across the wet grasses.

"Nothing here." Hod answered, and Walter's voice boomed from the right of the two men.

"Nothing here either, seems like an old shallow well, but nothing in it." Walter flashed his light beam upward toward the sky. His foot slipped and stones rocketed down.

He swore. "Almost fell in myself."

"Be careful." Hod's command was serious. "We don't need another casualty. It would be hard carrying anyone out in this weather." He flashed his own light back and forth over the ground surface, searching yet beginning to believe his theory was wrong, that Enough hadn't fallen into an old well, but that Robbie's stones meant the lake bottom. Not smart to be out here tonight, he thought. Time to get out of the swamp and woods and into some warmth. There would be blowdown in the woods going back along the trail, and men had been killed by falling trees. Hod was too smart to push any further.

"Let's give it up. I thought we might find him, but I guess I was wrong. We'll start again tomorrow."

The men turned and headed back over the trail. They were still within hearing distance, had Enough been able to speak. But his mouth gag still held, and there was no way he could call for help. For a moment, seeing lights flashing distantly above, he had felt his courage rising. But now, on the surface of the wet stones below the trail, Enough lay helpless. The rising water at the bottom of the old cistern might finish what the murderer had started. Enough Peabody needed help. He needed it soon.

Or he would be added to the list of victims of a clever, clever mind.

Chapter Twenty-Three

While the men searched the swamp edge, A.E. spread her bank application papers across the long kitchen table. Lee sat looking at the figures, the two women alone at the table as preparations for dinner were finished and Peggy had disappeared. Lee's eyes scanned the lines of the financial report, and she shook her head. All the while A.E.'s hands kept shaking, and Lee realized her friend was under more stress than she had thought. Maybe working on these papers would help them both. A.E. was supposed to deliver them to Walter tomorrow.

"Look." Lee sorted out the forms. "It's not too hard. We need a copy of your last income tax. And we need your invoices for the past year, your books, all the information. Then we'll make a list of repairs you need in the lodge. Chances are Walter will want you to get estimates from a couple of contractors or individual carpenters and plumbers so the bank can see the amount the repairs will cost. It's not that difficult. We just have to make a coherent package."

"Maybe for you." A.E. tossed her head. "I was brought up to be an artist, not an innkeeper. I sort of fell into this job, and I've never done it well. There weren't so many problems in the beginning, but things have gone downhill in the last few years. How can I show any income if there isn't any?"

"There has to be some." Lee sighed. "What you have to sell them on is potential. You only have a small mortgage on the lodge now, so there's lots of room. If you worked at it, you'd have more guests. The free advertising Mr. Wortham gave you has already helped."

"Maybe I don't want to be a lodgekeeper." A.E. fought all the way.

"Maybe I don't want to sell real estate. But you have to survive, A.E. You know, there's a lot of years gone by between the teen dreams and the present reality. I had this idea I wanted to be a hermit and write books. Then I married and traveled over all over Europe. Now I've come to a totally unexpected time

106

in my life when I find myself with a man I had no idea I'd ever meet, let alone want to live with. You spent two years in Paris. It must have been a shock to you to come back here and pick up after your mother. But you did, and here you are, and you just have to go forward. What's the option?"

"I'd rather go fishing."

"And I'd rather just ride my horses through the woods. But sometimes we have to compromise. There are choices. Get the lodge on a sound basis, and then you can going fishing. Or take part of each morning now and go out on the pond. It'll put you in a better mood for what you have to deal with every day. Walter jogs, I ride my horses, Hod walks in the woods. We each have our own solace."

A.E. was recalcitrant. "I don't like having guests."

"But you do it well. There's nothing like your Saturday night feeds. People come back to stay here. Look at Mr. Fremont."

"Dead." A.E.'s voice was hopeless.

Rain lashed against the kitchen windows. One of the old maple branches crashed against the corner of the lodge roof.

Lee shivered, her mind shifting from finances to the men out in the storm. "They shouldn't be out in the woods with this wind."

"If I didn't have the lodge, none of this would have happened." A.E. was determined to sink in grief. "Mr. Fremont wouldn't be dead, Enough wouldn't be missing—"

"A.E., grow up. There's no safe place. No absolutely for sure place. Stop feeling so damn angry and so sorry for yourself. Look at all the people who came to help today. And I'll bet every third one has some problem."

There was a long pause as A.E. placed her hands on the table in an effort to still the shaking.

"Were you a good artist?" Lee's voice was gentler.

"I think I might have been. I haven't held a brush in years." A.E.'s voice was low. Lee's words cut deep—how dare she invade her privacy?

"Well, why don't you start again? There couldn't be a more perfect setting. Try watercolor. Try sketching. But try. You know Motorboat's theory."

"His theory?"

"Yes. To do one thing for an hour and then switch to something else. Hod told me about it once. I'm continually surprised at who that man knows. Motorboat's trucks have hauled for him. But,the theory. It stops you from getting bored with what you do every day. So why don't you go fishing for an hour one day and maybe paint the next day for that hour. You'll feel better about having to run the lodge, and maybe you're not such a bad artist. You might sell some paintings. You had to learn something in Paris."

A.E. grinned. "I learned something in Paris, all right. I'm afraid some of it might shock you. O.K. I'll try a new approach. Help me get these papers ready for Walter tomorrow, and I promise I'll try to compromise. Incidentally, Lee, something is bothering me about Peggy."

"Peggy Canevari?"

"Um. There's something not quite right. She's worked here for two years, and I've seen a change. She seems so secretive. I'm sure she is seeing someone she shouldn't be seeing. Maybe someone married."

"Any idea who?" Lee looked thoughtful.

"No. She takes her afternoon time off and walks up on the mountain. I thought she might be meeting someone from Bryant Pond. Yesterday I saw Mr. Sherman, the guest who came Tuesday, hanging around her in the kitchen. He'd come in for a coffee refill. She should have brought the pot out to the table. And they had their heads together chatting about something. When I came in they looked a little flustered. At least, he did. Peggy was cool. He'd only been here four days. And he's supposed to be on his honeymoon."

"It could have been perfectly innocent. She has a bit of a reputation, but I'm inclined to think that is because she is young and pretty. You've been satisfied with her work, A.E.?"

"Always. Enough was sort of sweet on her." A.E. turned suddenly to the window. "The men should be back by now, shouldn't they? That wind is fierce. I'd better go see to the porch chairs and pull them back into the building."

They rose together, and A.E. opened the outside door to a wind that swirled the papers on the table. They pulled back the rocking chairs. The cushions had already been taken inside at the beginning of the storm.

"There's someone coming now." Lee's eyes spotted the slow methodical walk and knew it was Hod. How many times she had watched him coming through a woods path, every step calculated, no energy wasted, his eyes scanning the woods about him, hearing every sound, noticing every plant and tree. Lee never ceased to be surprised at his knowledge of the world around him. And sometimes, more surprisingly, at the outside world as well.

Motorboat shook his head as A.E. asked the question.

"If he's out there, he can't hear us. We found three or four of those old well sites or cisterns. No one down in any of them far's we can tell. Most of them filled in. I'm beginning to lose hope. Where's Dick?"

"He's getting a team up to go out to the stone cache. There are trees down on some roads. Phone wires are down. He said something about it was foolish to go out till the storm's over."

"He's right on that count." Hod wiped his face with the towel Lee brought to him.

"Walter, are you all right?" The tall, thin banker looked pale. He and Hod were probably in the best shape of all the men who had searched that day, but strain showed in his face and his hands were scratched from turning over blackberry canes near the well sites.

"I'm fine, A.E. But I'm going to go back to camp now. Business as usual tomorrow morning. Perhaps I can catch a ride with someone, my front tire is flat."

"I'm leaving now. If you want, I'll give you a lift, Mr. Desmond." Peggy was putting on her jacket while A.E. helped her with a bag of leftovers to take home. Peggy's small sisters still lived in the Silvertown area, and Peggy had not forgotten how it was to be hungry. Although she had escaped to a small apartment in Bethel, she made a weekly trip with groceries to Silvertown. Leftovers from the weekend, if there were any, were a special treat to the two young Canevari sisters, whose goals were to emulate their older sibling.

"Thanks." Walter took the bag from A.E.'s hands. Peggy opened the kitchen door to the outside storm, now turning into a real hurricane.

"This is September weather, not August. Don't forget we have an appointment tomorrow morning, A.E." Walter followed Peggy through the storm to her small Volkswagen.

"Motorboat, do you want to stay here?" A.E. made the gesture.

"No, I'll go back to the house on the outside chance he is someplace safe and will come home. I can make some business calls from there. But I'll check with Dick later and see what the next step is."

Hod, in a low aside to Lee, said two words. "The pond."

Lee was almost sure of the ending. Now, she gathered up wet clothing, put an arm about A.E. for a moment, and patted Motorboat's shoulder. Hod opened the door, and they bent their heads into the wind and rain. Motorboat followed the two cars, having also accepted a bag of muffins from A.E.

The lodgekeeper sighed, took one last look at the maple tree that looked as though it might lose another branch, and returned to the guests who were playing bridge and mahjong in the great room. The fireplace had rolled back smoke in the high wind, but the guests seemed to take this as part of the adventure and had not complained. The Shermans sat by themselves in one corner of the room, back from the fireplace, and seemed to be talking earnestly. Twice Chuck waved his hands, and once Debby shook her head. Whatever the conversation, it ended as soon as A.E. walked toward them.

"Do you often have storms like this?" Debby rose in deference to the older woman. "I had no idea it could rain so hard up here in Maine. I thought August was the perfect time to take a vacation."

"We do have storms, but this is exceptional. It'll probably blow itself out by tomorrow morning. The wind is so fierce I'm going to let the fire die down now. It back-drafts in this kind of weather." A.E. poked among the logs to hasten their burning.

It was nearly eleven now. A.E. seldom went to bed before her guests, even when they were out late. She would read in bed and be sure there were no cigarettes burning when everyone was in bed. She had posted no smoking signs for several years, but it was understood that a guest might smoke out of doors on the porch. Even then once in a while she found a cigarette butt in one of the upstairs bathrooms. The insurance on the lodge had increased yearly, and nonsmokers helped the policy.

The games ended. The guests began to slowly climb the stairs to their rooms, most of them stopping to thank A.E. for an exciting weekend.

Just as though I had planned it in advance, she thought.

The Shermans were the last to leave, and A.E. walked about to be sure all windows and doors were secure against the storm. She was wearier than usual when she climbed the stairs to the tower room and the daybed she kept there to nap on occasionally. Tonight she would sleep there. There was no light on the mountain. She stood watching for several minutes, but there was no repeat of the glow she had seen on Saturday night. Without even washing her face she stripped down and slid between the linen sheets, pulling a quilt up over her. The rain lashed harder at the tower windows.

In town, Dick sat in front of the sheriff's desk. Half-filled coffee cups were pushed to one side, and the two men considered a bulletin they had just received.

"It could be. We won't know until the medical examiner gets through with him, but it could be the same man. Manny Watrous it says. Worked part-time as a frycook in Winchester. Used to hang around a riding stable in that area. He hired out one of the horses two weeks ago, said he was driving up to Maine for a vacation and wanted his own mount. The stable's owner said he really didn't know too much about horses, but they gave him a pony that was trail safe. Used to be a circus pony, they said, good with children. Manny should have been back before now, but they said he called in and said he was staying up longer. The horse trailer came from the stables, the serial numbers match. One other thing."

"What's that?"

"He'd been up on charges of drug dealing twice. But it was never proven. Couldn't get any testimony against him. One thing, though. They are pretty sure he is a connection."

"A connection?"

"Between one of the heads on the East Coast and Canada. They've been watching him for some time. And they are pretty sure he was meeting someone in Maine."

CHAPTER TWENTY-FOUR

Sunday evening, late.

Dick was weary. Men from the sheriff's office had brought the body out from the stone cache in the storm, Dick's sudden decision late that night triggered by the thought that someone or something might move it. There was something Dick couldn't quite put his finger on. Something smelling of evil and damp—decay and stones. Stone, Robbie had said, and Robbie had been right.

Both Mr. Fremont and the man in the stone cache had been bludgeoned to death. And Enough was missing. The sounds of the storm mounted, and Dick, sitting in the sheriff's office, shivered.

He spent two hours going over the possibilities of Manny Watrous. Finally, exhausted with trying to figure it all out, at three in the morning he went home to Frieda, who was still awake but calmer. The two talked for another hour. Dr. Anna had given Frieda hope, the baby appeared to be able to go full term. Two school chums had dropped in that Sunday, and Frieda was beginning to feel like her old self. She even began to plan to cook breakfast for Dick, no more of this driving into the doughnut shop for coffee and two fat-laden puffs. For the first time in weeks they fell asleep in each other's arms, but those few hours of slumber didn't compensate when the phone rang at six o'clock. Monday was going to be a full day.

"Dick, I'm going back up there in about half an hour." Motorboat sounded wide awake. "I've been thinking about that pond."

"We're all going back just as soon as I can find my clothes and start up again." Dick's voice dragged. "I didn't get in until this morning. We brought the body out. And there's some new information on that man we think brought the horse up to Maine. I need to ring Hod—"

"No need, he's right beside me." Motorboat turned the phone over to the woodsman, who sat across from him in the kitchen of the little ranch house. "He showed up around five—came in and put the coffee on and made the best scrambled eggs you ever put your tongue around. He's right here."

Dick felt more alert. He was heartened to think these two would be searching with him today. For this was decision time: to drag the pond or not drag the pond, this had to be faced. And if the boy's body came up, then the search was over. An end Dick did not desire.

A few more sentences, the phone conversation ended, and Dick showered and dressed to come downstairs and find Frieda fussing with bacon and eggs and pouring coffee. He grinned. This was like the old days—maybe a baby wasn't going to be so bad after all. He made short work of breakfast, tweaked his wife's ear, and gave her a hug and a kiss. "I don't care how fat you get, just stay the same Frieda. And take a nap this afternoon. I'll call in sometime during the day, don't know how many we'll have out searching. A.E. will have food for us I'm sure. You just call Dr. Anna if you don't feel well, O.K.?"

Frieda nodded. It had occurred to her that she just might drive up to the lodge herself, she felt so good, might even see A.E. for a minute—they hadn't talked in several weeks. She hugged her husband back, gave him a pat on the cheek, and waved as he drove off in the cruiser. She'd totally forgotten to feel sorry for herself, her body felt more like its old self, and Frieda ventured a giggle as she piled frying pan and plates into the sink. She was tired of staying in bed all day, she would join the excitement. Her head full of her day's plans, she climbed the short flight of stairs in their bungalow to dress and make ready for the day.

Monday mornings Walter Desmond usually arrived early at the bank. He jogged at five-thirty, showered, and made his own breakfast. Carol and the children would still be asleep, if they were home. Walter drove to Bethel, stopping to pick up another coffee at the doughnut shop drive-through. He needed hot coffee to face his day at the bank. His secretary came in later than he did, and the office pot wasn't made until nearly eight-thirty.

He had been off certain days for the past week, taking part of his scheduled vacation at odd times because of the shortage of help in the mortgage department. In a small bank even the president filled in occasionally.

All the way up Route 26 he had been thinking about yesterday's search for Enough Peabody. It pleased the banker to think that his own body was still in good shape after the search through the woods and the mountain. Going back a second time through the wind and rain to the monument area had been proof of his fortitude. Better than that trucker, for sure. In fact, better than all the rest of the searchers, with maybe the exception of Hod Cole. Not a man he particularly cared for.

Walter needed to be one up, his life story was long on success, and his physical being was of prime importance. Last night, back from the search, he had showered, shaved, and then sat in front of the fireplace with his evening drink. Carol and the children were still in Boston. Tonight he would call them and see how long this blessed absence might continue. He would like to join the search party again today, but the bank needed attention and he'd had more time off recently than he'd planned. He sighed, took the cardboard lid off the coffee cup, and sipped thoughtfully. There certainly were mortgages enough to attend to. And, tomorrow, Tuesday, A.E. would be in again, this time, he hoped, with a financial statement in good order and legible enough for the bank to understand what she had in mind for that falling-down lodge.

If only she weren't so stubborn. And if only his life weren't so complicated.

Hell, if only pigs could fly.

CHAPTER TWENTY-FIVE

Monday morning.

A.E. rose early. The past week had been stormy, but now the valley seemed calm. The first cup of coffee gave her strength as she sat in her usual spot on the lodge steps at five-thirty. A trout jumped from the waters near the left shore, and her mind methodically recorded the fishing spot. Maybe tomorrow, no time for fishing today. She knew Dick and Motorboat would drag the pond, the last possibility. And find the boy.

Why? For a long time A.E. had been treading water, in a waiting place going through daily routines, the larger part of her trapped in an existence she resented, the smaller part dreaming of undisturbed solitude. Like a wheel out of balance, every rotation uncomfortable. But now the conversation with Lee came to mind. The loss of Enough, so young, only reinforced Lee's words— "Sometimes we have to compromise. There are choices. Take part of each day. Find your own solace."

So today would begin the change. Using time in a different way. Using life in a different way. Facing, as Lee had said, reality.

A.E. smiled. Like the bluebird, it had been right there in front of her. The pond might be Enough's grave, and there would be tears shed over that. It also might be her own salvation.

A long time ago, she thought, there was another world. I wonder if I've forgotten what I learned? I wonder if the paint box is still in the attic? Everything will be dried up by now. Chinese red and crimson, azure and midnight blue, the badger-hair brushes, the pad of watercolor paper, the charcoal and the sketch pencils. I haven't looked at that box in over twenty years, since the day I came home from Paris. It must still be there.

Willen is kunnen. She remembered the saying written on the wall of the Paris room. If you want to—you can.

114

Lee was right. How she used her life was her choice. She would start today.

At High Meadows, Lee, by herself after Hod had left early to join Motorboat, thoughtfully ate a small omelet, stacked her dishes in the sink, and with a second cup of coffee in hand, called Kate and walked to the barn to feed the horses and turn them out.

Last night in bed, she and Hod had talked about yesterday, the hunt for Enough, the storm, and the frustration of having to leave Indian Lodge with no successful conclusion to the search.

Hod had been puzzled. "There's just something I've missed, and I can't place what it is—I was so sure he might be in one of those old wells. Nothing left now but the pond, and you know, Lee, every instinct tells me he's not there. So, where is he? I feel like I'm losing my touch."

Lee's hand had stretched up to turn off the bed light. She slid down beside the woodsman and spoke softly. "You'll find the answer. You always do. Sleep now, tomorrow may be an even longer day."

It turned out she was right. In ways neither of them could imagine.

CHAPTER TWENTY-SIX

As A.E. sat facing the lake and Frieda cooked breakfast for Dick, Walter Desmond followed Route 26 to Bethel to start his day at Indian Head Bank.

And Enough, still breathing at the bottom of the cistern, renewed his courage. He was determined to escape from his stone prison. The water was no longer rising, the rain had stopped, and although every bone ached, hunger seemed to clear his mind. Enough forced himself to move in search of something sharp and found a sharp rock protruding from the cistern wall. He sawed the bonds holding his hands back and forth against a jagged rock until they finally gave way. It took only a moment to release the filthy head bandage and remove his mouth gag. Retching, he bent over and whacked his head against the stone wall.

He swayed as he stood upright. He was dizzy, and the darkness around him gave him no clue as to how deep in the earth he was situated. Reaching his hands up he discovered a small outcropping and swung himself toward the dim light. He fell back, injuring an elbow, and felt blood dripping down his arm.

"Robert Bruce," he muttered. "Good man."

Finally, ten minutes later, his hands found another rock and then another. The stone walls narrowed. There was a top mass of vines, roots, and what felt like a good-sized rock. It took some doing, but he finally crawled out into the open.

The air was clearing, the ground was still sodden, but he could see enough to know he was somewhere on the edge of the swamp and probably not too far from the burial cache of the unknown person. Someone must have searched for him. He recalled a light beam entering his prison, then drawing back. How long he had lain there was the question. What day was it?

He rested for a moment. His bones ached and he was still dizzy. Best to start back to the lodge—maybe the searchers would be out again and help him. He straightened up and pushed his way through bushes to try and pick up a trail. His head still felt like a hive of bees. He retched again, put his hand in his pocket, and pulled out the filthy head bandage, which, in the morning light, appeared to be navy blue in color. A bandanna, he thought, as he wiped his mouth.

Where've I seen that before?

At the Egglestons' Frieda changed into a denim tent dress, stuffing her still-swollen feet into socks and sneakers. She left the dishes in the sink. She walked through the breezeway to the garage and her car.

Attitude change, she thought, that's what I needed, an attitude change. I just wasn't looking at things in the right way. I got so caught up in my own body I forgot what else was happening. I'm going to drive up to the lodge and see A.E. Maybe I can help in some way.

She remembered Dick, last night, telling her of all the people who had come to help in the search for Enough. And there, she thought, is where I ought to be too. I can at least help A.E. make coffee.

The gas gauge was low, but there was probably enough to get to the lodge and back. She'd fill it later. Frieda made a decision she was later to regret. She backed out of the small garage.

Ten minutes later, driving along Rowe Hill Road, she rolled her window down to smell the fresh, crisp air of the pine woods.

I've been too long in my own depression, she thought. How could I let myself get into this state?

"You're going to be a fine, strong baby." She patted her stomach as she turned into the long dirt road leading to the lodge.

Something or someone stumbled into her path from the woods on the right-hand side. Frieda screamed. She hit the brakes, and the little car shook to a stop. Whatever it was crumpled in front of the car. Shaking, Frieda opened the door and stepped out to confront the boy rising from the dirt. The smell was overpowering, but the dirty, bruised face was the face of Enough Peabody. The voice was cracked and ragged, almost a cackle.

"Help."

Frieda gagged, stretched out her hands, drew them back, and then her heart took charge.

"Enough, my God what happened? Here, get in the car, I'm going to the lodge. We've got to get you some help. And call Dick right away. They are getting ready a team of divers to search the pond. They've been looking on the mountain for you for the last two days. Don't try to talk. Get in the car."

She opened the door, trying to ignore the stench and helped him in. Enough was moving, but just barely. Here, at last, was help. He had stumbled through the swamp and the woods, hoping to find a road, knowing he must be near one, but with not enough strength of mind to orient himself to his surroundings. Truth told, Enough was in bad shape.

They reached the lodge within minutes.

A.E. took one look at Enough. "Frieda, can you drive him right to the hospital? I'll follow immediately as soon as I call them and tell them you're coming. I have to tell Dick to call off the team of divers. I'll send Peggy to tell him you've found Enough. Are you O.K., Frieda? Can you handle this?"

Frieda nodded, turned the car, and headed back up the dirt road. Halfway up the narrow entrance road she was intercepted by Walter Desmond.

Thinking things over at the bank, he had called A.E. and decided to leave for an hour and watch the divers. His four-wheel drive nearly crashed into Frieda as they met coming around a corner.

There is a courtesy about camp and country dirt roads. There are always pullovers, places to pull to the side while the other car goes by. Every dirt road into a camp or cottage has a pullover. Without it there could be no two-way traffic. Frieda stopped and waited for Walter to back up to the nearest pullover.

"I have Enough." She leaned out of the window. "He's hurt, and I have to get him to the hospital. I'm in a hurry. Let me by, please."

Walter did just the opposite. He jumped from the four-wheel drive and came to Frieda. "Thank God you found him. Are you all right, Frieda? Let me help. There's more room in my car. Here, I'll carry him and you go straight to the hospital and say we're on the way. You can't lift him out. It will be quicker this way." The tall man scooped up Enough, who was almost comatose, and carried him easily to his own car. Backing up rapidly, he turned in the pullover and roared away up the hill.

Frieda was, in spite of all her good intentions, relieved. The fact was she had been terrified Enough would die before they could reach the hospital. A.E.'s decision had been correct, but Frieda hadn't been sure she could handle all this. What had started out to be an exploratory morning with her own feelings had turned into a nightmare in which she was responsible for someone else. Meeting Walter was a godsend. She followed the disappearing car as fast as she could, up to the main road, over Route 26. Then she lost him in traffic. And her car, spitting and choking, came to a halt.

"Darn. I'm out of gas." It had to be right now. Luckily she was close to the Bryant Pond station. She slid out of the seat and started to walk the few feet for help. Walter, by now, was well on his way to the hospital.

In a matter of minutes the man who owned the station was pouring gas into the small car. Helping Dick Eggleston's wife might come in handy someday.

"They find that boy they been looking for?" He shook the last of the gas drops off the funnel and tightened the cap.

"He walked out of the woods just half an hour ago. He's on his way to the hospital. That's where I'm going. I guess I ought to call A.E. and tell her I've been delayed. Or try to reach Dick. Could I use your phone?"

"Help yourself, right inside on the desk. Step careful now." He suddenly had a good look at Frieda. "You O.K.?"

"Oh, I'm fine. I'll just call the hospital to be sure he's there O.K." Frieda dialed the number.

At the large county hospital the emergency room had no record of an Enough Peabody being brought in. Dick Eggleston had called in a moment ago. And A.E. Gibbons. Both of them had reported he was on his way in. The only thing was, he wasn't there yet. And it was at least half an hour since Frieda had met Walter Desmond on the camp road.

Frieda felt a shiver run down her spine. Someone's walking on my grave, she thought.

Or on Enough Peabody's.

CHAPTER TWENTY-SEVEN

At the same time that Frieda and Enough were encountering Walter Desmond on the road to the lodge, Robbie was brushing Howard. The Swamper struggled with the still-matted coat of the Pony of America. For that is what Howard was, a breed developed after World War II from a cross between an Appaloosa mare and a Shetland pony. A sturdy, honest animal, ideal for trail rides and drawing carts, good with children and novice riders.

Howard was a roan, spotted in the manner of an Appaloosa, and thirteen hands high. This Monday morning, he was in friendlier hands than he had been two weeks ago. A former circus pony, he had been purchased by the owner of a riding stable in Winchester because he was docile and dependable with children and novice riders. When Manny Watrous wanted a safe mount for Maine, the owner of the stable knew Howard to be the correct choice.

Lee had suspected Howard's lineage when she'd picked up his hooves, dainty and striped, the clue to the Pony of America. His face showed so-called varnish marks, with the skin speckled around the nose. But people who owned an animal like Howard would be searching for him, and she had been puzzled. Why wasn't his owner out looking for him?

Robbie, as he brushed and wrestled with Howard's matted coat, was content just to be with the pony, reading his thoughts and talking with him. As great as his own mother's power to see into people's minds was Robbie's ability to see into the minds of animals. He had known immediately that Howard needed help, and he had helped him. Hadn't he buried the saddle dragging behind him, buried it deep in one of the old wells that dotted the area around the monument. That's where he had found Howard, struggling through the briars, dragging the saddle behind him, and Robbie knew instantly that panic filled the pony's heart and that he needed help.

Robbie had looked for whoever had been on the saddle. That is, he'd looked for a short span of time. As long as he could, holding the reins of the bridle, which had fallen to the ground and tangled around the pony's front left foot. The girth had loosened on the western saddle that was half hanging from the pony, dragging on the ground.

Robbie had unhooked the fastenings, taken off the saddle and bridle, and after standing for a while with the trembling pony, had decided to throw everything down one of the wells. Whoever owned this pony wasn't there, and Robbie was sure he didn't want to meet him.

Terror was written all over Howard. And terror was a subject Robbie didn't want to face. So he had simply destroyed any traces of Howard's ownership and led him , with one hand touching the pony's neck, and no lead line, through the swamp and back to his cabin. Asked by A.E. where Howard had come from, Robbie had not lied. There had been part of an old wire fence nearby, Howard's feet were near it.

He had not really lied. He simply hadn't told the whole truth. Only part. Swampers knew the ways of survival. Only tell what you are asked, never more. Possibly less.

Gently, his old brush soothed Howard's matted sides and gently he removed burrs, all the while humming in a soothing tone. He had done this every morning since he'd found Howard. The pony leaned sideways against the small man, enjoying the companionship and understanding.

For a horse knows, never think he doesn't. Kinship is there or it isn't. The link between horse and man, gently forged, may be forever.

This Monday morning Robbie was doing more thinking than usual. The problem facing him was how to feed Howard over the winter. Grain would be needed, and this was not a barter item. Luckily there were several finished baskets in the corner of the cabin and perhaps now was the time to give in to A.E. and Lee's suggestion of letting them place them in one of the galleries in Bethel.

"There's a market for them, Robbie. I know a gallery owner who can sell all you can make. Let me price them for you. People will buy baskets like yours. They are beautifully made. And the money can help you, even if you don't want it now. You can put it in the bank and have it later. Robbie, they are museum pieces—there are very few baskets that even come close to yours. Please think about it." A.E. had talked to a deaf ear.

But now Robbie was reconsidering. Howard's feed was important, and A.E. had said she'd help. And if the whole world went wrong, and he was put in jail, the money would help Howard. Robbie hummed and thought and brushed.

Slowly he reached a conclusion. He opened the paddock gate, branches woven together with grape vines, and guided the pony within. The blue cart stood nearby under a large maple, and Robbie pulled it forward, and then loaded it with baskets he brought from the interior of the cabin. A few had swing handles and were similar to small apple baskets, but the majority were

Robbie's signature baskets, long and low with a double row of lashing around the top and a graceful handle carved from a single piece of ash. They were stained a deep brown and had a mellowness hard to duplicate. These were the gathering baskets of old, the Swamper's heritage baskets, reminders of another day in the 1800s when the houses lined the swampís edge and the occupants made their living from their herbs, their baskets, and the land around Indian Pond.

Now, Robbie had someone to take care of, and he was no longer all alone. It would be a fair trade, as they say in the country, a fair trade, the baskets for Howard's winter rations.

He harnessed up the pony to the cart, closed the cabin door, and started off down the road toward the lodge. He took the dirt road that came out on Rowe Hill Road and then continued down into Indian Pond. It would be slow going, but Robbie had made his decision and he was on his way.

Meanwhile, at both the sheriff's office and at the lodge there was consternation. What had happened to Walter Desmond and Enough? The hunt for Enough had been called off, the hospital emergency room was alerted, but the two had disappeared as they say "from the face of the earth."

Sheriff's cars combing Route 26 hadn't turned them up. "Maybe there's been an accident. They're over a bank, and the car can't be seen. Get out and look in every ditch. They should have been at the hospital long ago." Dick felt an overpowering sense of doom, something was happening out of his control, and he suffered the frustration of not having a handle on the events.

Then he called Hod, who was getting ready to leave High Meadows for the lodge, not knowing Enough had been found.

Dick described the happenings in short order. Hod listened intently.

"Did Walter say anything when he picked up Enough from Frieda? What did Enough say? What did Frieda say?"

"Enough could hardly talk. He was in bad shape. Walter's taking him to the hospital was a big help, Frieda said. She was frantic because she was so low on gas. He just picked up Enough, put him in his four-wheel drive, backed up, turned around, and drove up the road. She followed him toward Bryant Pond and lost him when she ran out of gas. He had plenty of time to get to the hospital when she called there, but he hadn't come in. I'm confused, Hod, and I'm beginning to wonder. Could Walter have anything to do with this?"

Hod's answer was grim. "I've been wondering for the past few hours. Turns up at the most convenient times, doesn't he? But never mind that. The question is, where could he have gone off Route 26, and where is he now? More important, where is Enough? What does Enough know that Walter didn't bring him in? I think I might know the answer."

Dick held his breath. "Well, we better find them mighty soon. Enough isn't going to last too long without some help, if he's in the shape Frieda said he was in. Probably badly dehydrated, and it wouldn't take much to finish him off. And if it is Walter that's at the bottom of this, how come he didn't finish him off to begin with?"

"That we got to find out. Right now, I'll bet he might have taken Route 232, swung around to the road that comes back by North Pond, and doubled back to his camp or wherever he put Enough in the first place. That is, if it's him. Look, quit talking and let's move. I'll meet you up where 232 goes off of 26 in about 15 minutes. Let's follow that trail back. I'm guessing you have troopers all up and down 26."

"Yes, they're combing the main road. I didn't think of 232. You may be right. But how in hell does Walter figure in this? I'm going to check with the hospital one more time, put a man on there, and I'll meet you."

Hod agreed, put down the phone, and stood quietly for a moment, absently patting Kate Gordon's head and staring at the county map that hung on the kitchen wall.

What was going on here? Only Frieda had seen Enough, only Frieda had seen Walter take him. Surely Frieda wasn't involved, so that had to leave Walter. Hod recalled that Lee had mentioned Walter's wife being away with the children. That left Walter's camp empty except for Walter. And the camps in the same area were vacant this summer, according to Lee. So there would be no one around to hear Enough if he cried out, that is, if he was taken back to that area.

Hod left Lee a note, patted Kate Gordon's head again, and locked the kitchen door, after removing his rifle from the rack and putting it in the back of his four-wheel drive. Halfway up 26 he thought of the cisterns and wells and old cellar holes they had looked at in the rain the past night.

Had there been someone in one of them? Was Enough there then? If so, why hadn't they seen him when they shined their lights, or heard him if he called out?

Maybe they had. Maybe he hadn't, and Motorboat hadn't, but Walter had. After all, Walter said he looked down two of the holes. And would he say if he saw him?

Not, thought Hod, if he'd pushed him down there.

For sure, not. And maybe that was the connection.

It could be Walter, after all.

CHAPTER TWENTY-EIGHT

Monday morning the lodge dining room hummed with speculation. Peggy served breakfast to the Shermans and the couples that had come in on Saturday—buckwheat cakes with Maine maple syrup from Coopers, fresh apple tart with real whipped cream, and never-ending cups of hot coffee from the old-fashioned kitchen coffee maker. The guests had risen early to help take part in the search, but now A.E. announced it was called off.

"He's been found and is on his way in to the hospital. The search is over, and we're all so grateful to everyone who helped. I'm going to the hospital now, so lunch may be a bit delayed, but we'll make up for it with an afternoon tea and a celebration late dinner. There'll be coffee on in the kitchen all day, so please be at home while I'm gone."

A.E. felt the winds of relief blow over her. She had been surprised at herself—her distress over Enough and the search and her feeling of thankfulness for the help of people she did not even know who had come to the lodge, set up the food table, fed the searchers, and quietly faded away in the evening.

People she'd never met, people Motorboat had never met, but people who knew who they were in spite of that. There's a Maine saying, "Don't blow your nose too loud, the mountains have ears."

And heart, thought A.E. And heart.

The phone rang. A.E., talking with the Shermans, left it for Peggy to answer. She would need Peggy more than ever today—there was Nancy's room to get ready. Dick had said she might move into Mr. Fremont's room, and fresh bed linen needed to be taken from the big linen closet, the bathroom cleaned, and vases of flowers set on the little desk and the bedside table.

A.E. planned to attend to the flowers herself. First she had to drive in to the hospital to see how Enough was, then she planned to talk with Frieda. Probably Frieda had talked with Enough on the way to the hospital and she would know what had happened to him in the past two days.

A.E. cleaned plates away from one table, and hefting the big aluminum tray, swung open the kitchen door to find Peggy standing frozen by the phone, tears in her eyes.

"Peggy, what is it?" A.E. was concerned.

Peggy shook her head, wiped her eyes, and turned away.

"Nothing, I'm just tired from yesterday."

"Who called? Was it for you?"

"Look, I can't discuss this. Not now. I'm all right, A.E., really." The girl turned away and began to stack dishes.

The phone rang again, and this time A.E. answered. It was Dick, agitated and speaking fast. "He never reached the hospital. I've called Hod. Something is badly wrong."

"What are you talking about?"

"Enough."

"But he went into the hospital with Frieda. I'm just about to leave for town now."

"A.E., he never reached the hospital. Walter met Frieda, took Enough in his vehicle, and drove off for the hospital. Only they never reached there. We don't know what happened. They may be off the road somewhere along Route 26. Or on some other route. It's a puzzle, and Hod and Motorboat are going with me to see if we can find them. I have an all points out. That's why I'm calling you. Stay there, don't leave. Maybe they'll turn up there."

"Frieda?"

"She's fine. Just ran out of gas and so she lost them on Route 26. She'd been following them up until Bryant Pond. Never did keep that gas tank full like I've told her. She's back home. Dr. Anna's on her way over to see her. But we've lost Enough and Walter, and we haven't a clue to where they are. So, just stay there, will you? I'll call in soon."

A.E. hung up and stood motionless in the center of the old kitchen. "I wonder—"

"Peggy—" The girl had disappeared.

A.E. walked out on the long front porch and looked in both directions. No Peggy. Then she turned back into the hallway running behind the kitchen and leading to the dining room. She looked into the under-the-stairs bathroom with the still-to-be-fixed doorlock, and frowned. It wasn't like Peggy to just disappear, she took her work seriously. There was an unspoken agreement between Peggy and her employer that sometimes after a particularly difficult week there was some extra money in the pay envelope. A.E. had always treated her well, much better than any former employer, and Peggy was grateful. No, it was not like Peggy to just disappear.

A.E. hesitated at the bottom of the stairs. The only possible place Peggy might have gone was the room on the third floor that was her own. She had been in tears. Maybe, whatever it was, it just needed a little thinking through and she needed to be alone. The dining room bell rang, and A.E. turned and walked again down the long hall. She entered to serve more coffee to the Shermans. Her eyes scanned the tables—there was more to do and she momentarily put Peggy's whereabouts aside.

On this same Monday morning Old Bill had been doing a bit of cogitating, as he put it. He had been puzzled since Sunday, when he had returned to his camp in the driving rain. Enough's whereabouts were a mystery, but more so was the reason for Mr. Fremont's murder. Hod had told Bill that the man in the cache and Mr. Fremont had both died in the same way, with a blow to the back of the head. Robbie's mallet sans Robbie on the other end, had probably killed Mr. Fremont, and a large stone had done in the unknown man in the stone cache. But why?

Bill had served a long term in jail, and he'd seen and heard most everything. By now he had come to the conclusion that Mr. Fremont's death had not been planned. His old friend must have found something he was taking down to the lodge. Only an unusual happening would have distracted his digging. Whatever it was must have been of some importance to someone else, someone who could not allow discovery. Therefore, the murder from behind and the total lack of connection between the murderer and murderee. Except for that one thing, the item or items he'd found. So what could that be?

Bill puffed and rocked and thought. The man in the cache was not from the area, according to Dick and Hod. There was a possibility he'd come in on a horse. Robbie'd found a horse. Now, why a horse? If the man wanted to meet someone on the mountain he might need transportation, and he wouldn't want to be seen or heard. So, no mountain bikes, those noisy obscenities.

So you had Mr. Fremont, who Bill by now was convinced was an innocent party, a loose horse, and a man who had most definitely been killed by a blow on the back of the head and then buried by someone, whoever that was, in the stone cache.

And then Enough, seemingly spirited away to wherever he was, which probably was someplace on the mountain. It all seemed to revolve around the mountain—and, Bill thought, suddenly leaning forward in his chair—the mountain and the caves. The caves.

For Mr. Fremont, and for Bill, a possible Indian hiding place, a possible place for the shaman to consult his gods, to talk with the spirits of the animals, and to find a way to help his people. A place for good.

But, for someone else, someone in our own time? Bill's eyes narrowed. A hiding place, for sure. No one would ever find what might be hidden, and maybe it didn't have to be hidden for long. Only Mr. Fremont with his inquisitive spade. And that led to his death.

Again, Bill moved in the chair, repositioned his legs on the porch floor, and leaned forward.

"Money," he breathed the word, and then said it louder. "Money." You might not kill for a small item, a piece of pottery, a shard, an arrowhead. But you would kill for money. Hidden money, someone's hoard. From what?

And Bill, smart in the ways of the prison world, thought he might know. Today he lived a life of quiet and peace, but he still remembered ghosts. He spun a story in his mind, and he was fairly close to home base. A drug connection, money exchanged, money hidden and money found. Reason enough to kill if Mr. Fremont exposed what he had found. And probably was on the way to do so, when someone, someone who couldn't afford to be exposed, killed him. That had to be it.

"So," mused Bill aloud, "it stands to reason that man buried in the cache knew something too, and Enough stumbled on his body. Three people don't all die on the same mountain by chance. Somebody couldn't afford to be exposed. And that somebody is our man. Or woman, as it may be. That somebody had to be the drug connection."

Bill sat about ten minutes longer. He downed another cup of coffee strong enough to excite his ulcer and decided on a course of action. The lodge was the logical place to go. He wasn't quite sure what his mind had come up with, but after all he had moose wisdom, hadn't he? He remembered the years talking with Indians on the plains, teaching them in the Arizona school. And what they had taught him—the animal ways, the totems they revered. Maybe he had second sight, maybe like Robbie he could see within the mountain.

Like Robbie. Now Bill's direction was sure. He needed to talk with Robbie, to talk with A.E. So, not knowing that Enough had surfaced and then disappeared again, Bill picked up his staff and set out for the lodge.

His legs ached. He would not take the road over the mountain, but the road on the north side of the pond, by the camps.

Where Walter Desmond, at the same time, was depositing Enough in one of the empty cabins, Enough bound and tied again, this time to stay. There would be time to dispose of him later. For now, every moment counted. Peggy should be here soon, the coffee can had to be dug up out of the garden, and they would leave.

But not before he had disposed of Enough for good and all. No need to implicate Peggy, she had a soft heart.

Walter Desmond had made his choice. He had killed twice, he could kill again. It was beginning to be easy.

CHAPTER TWENTY-NINE

Lee, returning from an early visit to the office, had given up all thoughts of real estate this Monday morning. Hod had left her a note to tell her in three short sentences that Enough had been found only to vanish for a second time. Now, standing in the kitchen of the old farmhouse, Lee thoughtfully considered what she might be able to do to help.

"The lodge," she spoke aloud. "I'm not on duty this afternoon at the office. No appointments. A.E. must be frantic with all the people in and out and maybe I can help there. If I can get up Route 26 through all the roadblocks, I can spend the rest of the day there. Hod and Dick and Motorboat are bound to end up at the lodge."

She changed from office clothing to jeans and a light sweater. The breeze portended October rather than August, and on the pond it would be cooler. She ran a comb through her hair and patted Kate's head as Hod had done a few hours before.

"You need a walk first, old girl. Patience." And she took the leash from the entry wall and motioned to the outside door. The orchard trees bent low with their burdens, and the sound of voices singing in the lower orchard reminded Lee that the Jamaicans had arrived that morning. They were pleasant family men, and Lee welcomed each apple season when she would again greet them. For ten years the same ones had returned to pick apples for the man who ran the orchards for Lee. She smiled as she heard the voices and whistled up Kate for a short walk in the hardwood stand.

Fifteen minutes later she locked the door of the farmhouse and began the drive to Indian Lodge. She was stopped only once, the trooper, who was a friend, telling her that so far there was no trace of Enough or Walter Desmond or the car Walter was driving. It was beginning to look as though there was an out-of-state connection. The man in the stone cache had definitely been identified as Manny Watrous, a member of a drug ring. There were rumors someone in Maine was handling big money.

About to turn from Rowe Hill Road into the camp road leading to Indian Lodge, Lee saw a distant figure plodding along from the other direction. She stopped and waited until she finally recognized Old Bill, marching methodically along with the help of his applewood staff, evidently with the same destination in mind. She waited until he was within hearing distance and offered him a ride.

"Are you going to the lodge? How about a ride?"

"Thankee." Bill pulled himself into the car, settling into the seat with a sigh. "My bones aren't the bones they used to be. Thought I'd go see if I could do anything to help. Heard Enough was found and now he's gone again. What's going on here, Ms.Heaward? I've been thinking on this. What I'm coming on to is I think all this is connected. I believe my old friend found something on that mountain, something he was taking back to the lodge. And then someone just crept up behind him and killed him. From what the radio had to say of the man in the stone cache, he's a drug connection from Massachusetts. Then Enough gone. It doesn't smell right to me. Somebody can't afford to let it be known they are involved. Don't you think?" Bill settled back in the car and adjusted his seat.

Lee hadn't started up again. Listening to Bill's thoughts travel in the same direction as Hod's and Dick's, she felt a cold chill.

"It was Walter Desmond picked him up from Frieda, Bill. I can't believe Walter is involved. I've known him pretty well for years, and A.E. and Dick and Frieda went to school with him."

"Money." Bill snorted. "Maybe not, but funny he's missing too, according to what they said on the news just before I left. Had a bulletin out for them. It's noon now. If they are off the road, they should have been found. Not too many places on Route 26 where you can roll a car and not be seen if someone's hunting for you. I just came by the camps on the north shore. Didn't look like there was anybody around. There was a Volkswagen in one of the driveways, had a Maine license. Maybe one of the owners is up from Kittery."

"A Volkswagen?" Lee frowned, she knew the three absent owners and all had four-wheel drives, most drivers going in and out of camp roads these days had learned enough about Maine driving to invest in year-round vehicles.

"Maybe someone's switched cars." She turned into the gravel drive leading to the lodge. "Can I help you out, Bill"

"No, thankee, that little ride renewed my strength." Bill bowed slightly to the woman he'd come to respect and turned to the thin, wiry redhead that had long been a friend.

"Thought I'd come over, A.E. and see what's going on. I heard about it on the radio this morning. Any sign of them?"

A.E. shook her head. "Dick just called again, they are still searching. They're looking over on the camp side of the pond, now. Walter's camp and the others. He said they'd be back here in about half an hour. They may also try the old farm back in where they found the horse trailer."

"Well, someones up at the camps. Just saw a Volkswagen. Don't mind if I do." Bill took the offered cup of coffee from A.E.'s shaking hands. "You're shaking a bit, A.E. Just like your mother. Better lay off that coffee."

A.E. stared at the old man. "My mother? She shook too?"

"I used to come over to the lodge once in a while. Knew Susan the year before she died. Her hands would be shaking sometimes, said it was a family inheritance, I remember her saying. Used to take some medicine for it, she did. Some herb stuff. I recall Robbie's mother fixing it for her. Some woman, she was, Robbie's mother. Knew every plant and herb and tree in the forest. If she was alive, we'd know where Enough was. She could look into the mountain."

A.E. turned to Lee. "Peggy's gone."

"Peggy?"

"She just disappeared in the middle of breakfast. I've just finished cleaning up the kitchen. I don't know what I'm going to do with both Enough and Peggy gone. Lee, I'm scared, I'm really scared. There was a light on the mountain Saturday night. And I just went up to Peggy's room. Her clothes are gone and her purse. Her uniform is just laid across the bed. It's not like her to do that. Lee, what is going on?"

"I don't know. Bill, did you say you saw a Volkswagen over at one of the camps? With a Maine license plate?"

Bill nodded, sipping his coffee after lacing it with sugar. He dunked a doughnut methodically and thought for a moment. "Right by the third camp. Tucked in behind sort of. Why, what you getting at?"

"Peggy has a green Volkswagen." A.E. stated. "That was the only car, Bill?"

"Far as I could see."

"I need to tell Dick this." A.E. turned to the phone, but that moment the police car containing Dick, followed by Hod and Motorboat in Hod's car, drove into the dooryard. A few minutes briefing, with Bill's recollection of time and sighting, and the three men decided to head back to the north shore.

"We just came from there. No sign of anything, no cars or people. The camps are all closed and boarded up. Walter's is closed. Evidently his wife and children aren't back from Boston yet. There's no sign of anything wrong, just looks like he's in town at work. We peeked in the windows. Everything is ship-shape inside. No signs of any struggle." Dick was puzzled.

"We might have missed something." Hod, generally the last to speak, was thinking hard. "Now, how come Bill saw a car, we didn't, Peggy's missing and she has a green Volkswagen and it was a green Volkswagen Bill saw. What's our time factor, here? And how come she was there?"

"She had a phone call," A.E. suddenly remembered. "And she looked upset.

She was crying. I left her to go into the dining room, when I came back into the kitchen, she was gone. I thought she was upstairs, maybe upset about something in the family. But now, I don't know."

"She been going with anyone?" For the first time Motorboat spoke. His hand rested momentarily on A.E.'s arm, the touch gentling the shaking and somehow soothing the tall redhead. "Hear her mention any names?"

"No, but I think she was seeing someone. I tried once to talk with her. I thought it might be a married man and someone she couldn't talk about, but she cut me right off. None of my business, she said, and I suppose she was right."

"Maybe none of your business then," Dick mused. "But our business now. If it was Walter and she had a phone call from him and then went to meet him, that could explain it. Where's the green Volkswagen now? Where's Walter and more important, where's Enough? You know, Hod, you had a point when you said that Enough could have been right there, at the old house sites last night, only Walter might have foxed us into thinking he'd checked some wells and cellar holes and there was no one in them. But Enough was there all the time. So, now we just looked all around those camps. Maybe Enough is there, maybe Walter's outfoxed us again. I think we better add Peggy to our all points and go back there again just for a second check."

"Well, he's not my type, but I'm trying to figure what Walter has to do with all this? The man has everything you could want—money, a camp, a town house, a good job." Motorboat shook his head. "Why does he want to hurt Enough, if it is Walter? Don't make sense."

"Makes good sense," Old Bill interrupted. "It's an old proverb, more you have more you want. And there's just three ways to get money—you inherit it, you make it, or you steal it. I learned that a long time ago. Hasn't changed any since the beginning of time. Now, you take this Walter. Good job, but banking still doesn't pay an awful lot considering the responsibility. Got a wife and three kids and if I heard right two of them are heading for college soon. Didn't he say they were in Boston buying school clothes? Well, if somebody offered him a chance to make big money without taking too many chances, he might just decide to do it. Might not be probable, but anything is possible. If I thought on it long enough, I could make a good story out of this."

Hod had been silent for a long time, listening to the old woodsman's theory. Now his eyes narrowed and he studied Bill's face. "And if you and I think alike, where would a fox go? If he was that smart a fox from the beginning of the story?"

"Right back to his lair, after he'd led us all a merry chase for miles and in the wrong direction. Right back to his lair." Bill's voice was strong and sure.

"That's what I believe too. Let's go back there, Dick, and try again. I think we might have overlooked something."

Dick was troubled. They'd done this once, walked around all the camps, looked in Walter's windows, there was no life there that he could have seen, and he hated to miss anything. Maybe having Frieda on his mind was dulling his senses, he had found his mind wandering at times thinking of her and of the child that was coming. Was he losing his touch? Here was this old woodsman, probably with at least two jelly glasses of Jack Daniels in him even at this time of day, and he was spinning a possible scenario that Dick hadn't yet put together. Well, nothing to do for it but allow that Old Bill could be right. Better go back and check again.

"O.K., we'll go back. Let me make a call first, I want to be sure nothing's come in at headquarters and that roads are still to be checked all through the state. Looks like we have three people we're looking for now—Walter, Enough, and Peggy. What was she wearing, A.E.?"

A.E. shook her head. "I'm not sure, because when I saw her this morning she had her uniform on. She usually has on blue jeans with some kind of sweater top. And an old barn jacket, denim-colored, I think it is. Except for some days when she wears a skirt. I just don't know for sure."

"Well, I'll get out a description. I hate to think of Peggy mixed up in this." Dick strode inside to the hall phone.

"Motorboat—" A.E.'s voice trailed off. "I can't handle all this. First Enough, now Peggy."

The overly stout trucker methodically shifted his stomach over his belt buckle and hitched up the sagging jeans.

"Given a choice, it's Enough I want to find alive. And if it turns out Walter had anything to do with it, somebody had better be my keeper."

"No." Old Bill's voice was grim. "No. My keeper. Alexander Fremont was a good man. If it's Walter, I'll do the squaring up."

CHAPTER THIRTY

Walter had never intended it to end like this. Several years ago when he had met a Boston businessman at a bankers' convention in New Hampshire, they had discussed the rigors and stresses of the banking world. When he had been approached at the end of that convention to transmit a small package every so often from an unknown to an unknown, under cover of his own respectability; when he had considered the considerable amount of money offered for this service and the guarantee of anonymity; when he had weighed what the additional money might mean in his life, a final escape from a world he had never liked; when he considered all the factors, Walter, who in fact was a gambler at heart, decided that this was the only way to reach a goal he had set for himself, a goal of total disappearance into another world less stressful.

In short, a new identity in another part of the world.

Preferably on a small island in the South Pacific, and preferably with an agreeable companion.

The agreeable companion had come to mean Peggy Canevari. Peggy had dreams herself, and Walter appeared to be a means to an end. How he planned to do all this, she did not know, although she suspected. The fact that Walter's hands transmitted packages from one banker to another at the conventions, the fact that Walter had to travel on bank business, and the fact that he never spoke of any of this did not bother Peggy. She had long ago learned the value of the unspoken word. Walter never asked her about her own past and who she went with in the present. She never asked him about his family. They enjoyed their moments together in the way men and women have enjoyed each other for ages. Only once did he mention that he had future plans for both of them. Peggy agreed in theory and let it ride. Even her vivid imagination had never shown her where this was leading.

Now, watching Walter dig among his cabbages, Peggy was confronted with the reality of her situation. No longer a dream of what might be, this situation was immediate. Walter intended to go away now, taking with him whatever he had been hiding all over the mountain for the past two years. And he intended taking Peggy—if she still desired to go.

Three things were in Peggy's mind as she watched Walter methodically wipe dirt off the large coffee tin and peer into the interior.

Where was Enough?

What shape was he in?

Did she really want to go with Walter?

Peggy shivered and drew her denim barn jacket closer around her thin shoulders. Much as she cared for Walter, and she did care for him, more than any man she had known so far, much as her future might depend on it, she had to ask some questions. And she had to ask them now.

"Walter." She knelt down beside the thin man with the troubled face. He was methodically counting large bills that had been taken from their oilskin wrapping. "Walter, where is Enough? What does this have to do with you? I don't understand. Did you have anything to do with Mr. Fremont's death? Walter, I have to know."

Walter sighed and stuffed the money back into the can. He snapped the lid shut and rose from among the cabbages.

"Peggy, what's happened has happened. I never intended it to go this far. Mr. Fremont found the can. I met Manny Watrous two weeks before and told him this was the last time. He said I couldn't get out of it now, there was no way. I either kept on making the connection, or they would kill me. He might have done it then. So I had to get rid of him. By the time this gets back to the Boston end, I'll be out of here and in another country. Now, you can go with me or not, just as you please. I hope you will. But we have to go now, immediately. I'll leave the four-wheel drive here where it's hidden behind the camp. We can climb over the mountain. Then we can follow trails on the edge of the woods that go up to Bethel. We can pick up my other car there and head for Canada. After that we're on our way."

"It's five miles to Bethel. We're going to walk?" Peggy stared at him.

"Who would possibly think we would walk?" Walter sighed. "Where's your imagination? We'll walk all night just skirting the road, pick up the car, and take all the back routes. I know them all, so do you. Carol isn't back yet, the house is closed to all eyes, and its the camp they'll be searching, not the house. Peggy, people never think of the unexpected. That's why this was such a good connection. Who would suspect Walter Desmond?"

Peggy stared at him. "No one. And I can walk five miles. I can understand Mr. Fremont and I can understand the drug connection. Manny, did you say his name was? But Enough? Where is he? Surely you can let him go."

Walter sighed again. "I don't think so, Peggy. I don't know what he saw, what he knows. His problem was being at the wrong place at the wrong time. He found Manny's body, you know. And I couldn't take a chance on his telling the others where the body was. I don't know how much he saw when Mr. Fremont died. He was on the edge of the meadow. No, Enough has to go. He's in the last camp down. I'll just be a minute and then I'll be back. Stay out of sight, go back to the Volkswagen where the cars are hidden."

He reached out and touched her arm to pull her toward him, but Peggy, suddenly sobbing, broke away and ran toward the third camp.

"Peggy, don't make me do this." The voice was chilling. This was a different Walter. This was a man to fear. This was a man who pointed a gun at her.

Peggy turned and stared at the thin man with the gun in his hand. For a moment she stood sobbing, and then, with sudden decision, she turned away from the camp steps and walked back down the road to where the Volkswagen was hidden behind a screen of bushes.

Walter put the gun in its holster and started up the camp steps. Behind him, the Volkswagen backed out of the bushes with a roar, spun its wheels, and shot along the dirt road.

Only not in the direction of Rowe Hill Road.

But, with accelerated speed, directly into Indian Pond.

CHAPTER THIRTY-ONE

It is hard to make a decision when you're halfway down a road. It is hard to admit you might have made a wrong decision. On one hand was the fact that Walter had, by his own admission, killed twice and was about to do it a third time. On the other hand this man offered her a chance for a new beginning, a life with all her wants attended to, one with no money worries and one away from this small town area that she hated so much. Life on a beach in a warmer climate could be good, and Peggy, whose own morals at times had been twisted, was tempted. But there was another Peggy, the one whose small-town morality kept cropping up in corners of her mind. The Peggy who didn't want harm to come to that nosy boy, the Peggy who knew that, in spite of the drudgery of her life, there was something to be said for honesty.

So Peggy, who was a good swimmer and who also could take chances, and who had to face the reality that if she didn't join Walter he might kill her, this Peggy revved up the Volkswagen and shot off into the lake. There was a good chance she could get out, swim underwater, and reach the shoreline where the land jutted out to form a peninsula. Heavy woods growth might be able to hide her from Walter.

Time counted with him. He had to move quickly and perhaps she had the advantage of surprise.

Maybe the spirit of the pond spoke to Peggy in this moment of decision. Maybe the ghosts of Indians who had walked these shores gave her courage. At any rate, the Volkswagen shot into the lake with Peggy in it and sank within minutes.

Walter was dumfounded. Whatever he had expected, it wasn't this. He watched the pond, moving toward the shoreline, and waited for the girl to surface.

He could not wait long. In the distance was the sound of a car coming down the road toward the camps. Walter had to make a decision quickly.

Hastily he melted back into the woods behind his cottage, taking the coffee can with him. He was not far from where his own four-wheel drive was hidden. Whoever this was would probably not stay long, and when they were gone he'd finish off Enough and be on his way. Peggy would have to drown. He could not watch the pond any longer for motion. He had to completely alter his plan and get out the area. If she did survive, she'd tell his plan to Dick and some of those idiot troopers, so, just in case, he'd try a new tack.

For Walter this had now become more than a gamble. It was a game to be played to the finish, and he did not intend to lose. He had come too far, and success was too close. He did not intend to be bested. Hadn't he always won? His setters were the best, his saddlebred mare the finest—he wondered if the family would keep Katura or sell her.

Well, there were other horses, other parts of the world. He had always wanted to see the horses in Ireland. When he'd changed his identity maybe Ireland would be an option. The money in the can would take care of him for a lifetime.

He melted into the background of woods, and moving fast, took the trail toward the monument and Indian Lodge.

Hod, out of the car behind Dick, stopped to look at the lake. Years of living close to the woods and waters had fine-tuned his senses, something on the lake's surface seemed different. An ever widening circle on the water imprinted itself on Hod's narrowed eyes.

"Something just went in over there. Good-sized I'd say."

"Probably a fish jumping. No sign of any cars. Let's try the Desmond camp again first off, then see if we can get inside the other three camps. I just get the feeling there's something we missed." Dick half trotted up to the wooden deck in front of the Desmond camp, overlooking the lake.

"Door's locked, we don't have a warrant, but maybe we're just going to overlook that. Motorboat —?"

Motorboat had stopped to join Hod, who still stood puzzling over the pond's waters.

"Looks like there's some object there, a ways out." Hod pointed. "Could be a car top I'm seeing. What do you think, Motorboat?"

"Think we might could look. I want to see into those three camps first, though. We're close, Hod, I can feel it, and I hope we're in time. Enough was in bad shape, according to Frieda and A.E."

Dick, by now inside the Desmond cottage by means of a credit card to open the lock, knew full well he wasn't playing according to Hoyle, but then look who he was dealing with. By now he was pretty sure it was Walter he was looking for. He hadn't figured the motive yet, but it certainly looked as though

Walter had taken Enough for a reason.

The camp yielded nothing, except for the fact that a change of clothes for Walter was laid out in what must have been his bedroom. Dick noted that the adjoining bedroom appeared to be his wife's—they did not seem to occupy the same bed. But nowhere in the camp was there any sign of Enough.

Hod and Motorboat prowled about the remaining two camps, waiting for Dick to emerge from Desmond's. Hod's eyes noted dust and grime on the doors of one of the cottages and what appeared to be a cleaner area around the doorknob of the third.

"This one—" he motioned to Dick—"this one first."

Dick did not question. He'd by now come to trust Hod's instincts. Circling the camp, they found one window that seemed loose, and with Hod's expert maneuvering it was soon open with the three men helping each other inside.

There, bound and gagged, Enough, still alive but in bad shape, made a small motion of greeting. By now he was not a joy to sensitive nostrils, even his own.

Motorboat, whose car had followed Dick's cruiser to the camps, turned up the dirt road and headed fast for Route 26 and the hospital. On hand was on the wheel while the other reached back to pat Enough, who was curled up in a fetal position with his eyes closed.

"Take it easy, boy, I'm with you now. Just hang on." The words we need and wait for. The words Enough had pinned his hopes on. From the man he had always been able to count on.

In sad circumstances for a race car driver, but safe at last, Enough hung on.

CHAPTER THIRTY-TWO

It was Lee who helped A.E. with the kitchen cleanup and bedmaking of the occupied rooms at the lodge. Together they made up Nancy's bed in Mr. Fremont's old room, and together, having finally finished the preparations for the evening dinner, they dragged A.E.'s old easel, not seen in many years, down from the attic. The bamboo was filthy, and Lee fetched Murphy's Oil Soap and rags from the pantry. A.E. followed, carrying the paint box. She laid it gently on the kitchen floor and began to lay out the tubes of oil paint, the crayons, the pencils, the brushes, memories of her days in France crowding into her mind.

"I didn't see any canvas up in the attic, A.E." Lee rubbed the legs of the easel.

"I think there is some—in fact there's some stretched, I believe. Undercoated. I just remember packing everything up when I had to come home. It all happened so quickly when Mother died. Look at the jumble in this paint box."

"Didn't you ever paint here in Maine?" Lee rubbed briskly.

"No, it was as if a door in my life had closed. I started a couple of times, went up in the attic and just stood and looked at the easel, but that's as far as I went. I didn't care anymore. It seemed like all the energy went into taking care of the lodge. And then I dug some worms in the garden one day and just went out and fished."

"Fished." Lee repeated.

"Fished. It's peaceful on the pond, and nobody bothered me or asked for any more coffee or why the toilet didn't work. What happened to me, Lee? I just didn't care anymore."

"The same thing that happens to a lot of us, I guess. But you can start again."

"First of all I have to find out about Enough. Where he is, and where Peggy's gone to. I can't possibly run this place without help, let alone have time to paint."

Her fingers explored the depths of the paint box.

"Look, here's Crimson Lake. That was one of my favorites. The cap's on tight. I'll bet it's still fluid."

"See." Lee smiled. "You're beginning to think differently already. No more of this 'can't do.' You'll find a way. Whatever happens, you can close down for a while if necessary, but whatever happens you have to begin a new program. Block out that hour or so each day for yourself. What do you want to do first, pencil sketches or an oil? How about doing Motorboat fishing in your canoe?"

A.E. laughed. For the first time she began to have faith in her own ability.

"I dumped him out of that canoe once. That's exactly what I'm going to do, a picture of him fishing. Lee, the whole day seems better. Listen, I thought I heard a car. The men should be back soon."

The lodge guests were following their after-lunch pattern of sunning on the beach in the heat of the late August rays. One couple had gone upstairs to nap but the other two were stretched in beach chairs, faces upward under large-brimmed hats. Whatever was happening in the inner recesses of the lodge had not affected them. They were aware that the hunt for Enough had been called off,and there seemed to be some difficulty in finding exactly where he was, but none of this was of great importance in their lives. The three couples were only booked for a few more days. They had come to rest and look at the pond. Their own comfort was of greater importance than any happenings around them.

A.E. had thought fast even while she sorted paints. She had plenty of food in the freezer. Lee had offered to take a day or so off and help, and between them they could manage the bare essentials of keeping the dining room running.

"Hod's off with Dick, anyway," Lee had said, "and I can tell he's beginning to get the scent. Whoever killed Mr. Fremont and that man in the cache has no idea of Hod's ability to solve puzzles. I think he's getting close. So I might as well help you. Tom and Ellen are back now and they can take care of things during the day. I can help you with serving meals here until Peggy comes back."

"If she comes back." A.E. frowned. "I am totally at sea on this whole thing."

While the two women talked and sorted paint tubes, Old Bill rested off to one side in the shade of the porch. He rocked to and fro, thinking of the three men who had gone to the north shore camps and wondering what was happening. He had wanted to go, but he knew he would have been in the way. He moved slower than the younger men, and he felt in his bones that they were close to solving the puzzle.

Anyway, thought Bill as he rocked, Hod is close. I noted that look in his eyes, narrowed and angry. Whoever did all this didn't count on Hod Cole.

Robbie walked slowly behind Howard and the cart. He had stopped a few times to rest, for in places the path was narrow. He had decided to come through an older woods path that he had not used for some months. It was afternoon now, and he had started out in the morning. It was cool under the trees in the woods. They were beginning to reach the opening that led into the meadow from the other side of the hardwood stand. He rested Howard again, patted his head, and found a spare carrot which the pony neatly accepted.

Somewhere, on the other side of the hardwood stand, near the area where Mr. Fremont had been found, Robbie saw movement. The yellow tape was still in place in that area. Today there was no breeze. The sun was hot here on his head as well as on the heads of the bathers on the beach, but Robbie was almost sure he had seen movement in the bushes.

Deer, he thought. Close in for daytime though, they ought to be staying cool in the deep woods. He stood very still, conscious that both he and Howard were out in the open and could be seen from the other side. He waited.

On the north shore, Hod and Dick had searched all three closed camps and had found no one besides Enough. Motorboat, from the hospital, called Dick's car phone to say that the boy would be all right, although he was very dehydrated.

"Stunk more than anything else. Closest thing to a skunk I've been up to in a long time. Had them gasping in the emergency room. But he'll be all right now. He doesn't know much, just that after he saw a foot sticking out of the cache, someone grabbed him, and he must have been thrown down one of those old wells. Got out of there finally by himself. And walked out to the road where Frieda found him."

"Did he recognize Walter Desmond? Was he aware he was in a different car?" Dick was looking for some clue.

"Said he didn't know much of anything. Some man just picked him up and carried him. Next thing he remembers was being tied and gagged again. He just kept going in and out of a daze. He knew he smelled so bad he thought maybe he was dead. I'm going to stay here a while to see him when he's settled down. They said I could go back in. He has a private room. Any sign of Walter?"

"No," Dick answered. "We're still looking." While Dick was talking Hod's eyes were scanning the lake's surface. There was no breeze. The lake was calm. The afternoon was heating up. Hod, hunkered down in a shady spot beside the water, was thinking.

Bill had said he'd seen a Volkswagen. When the three men had come to the lake the first time there was no Volkswagen. And no Volkswagen the second time. But Bill had seen one. Peggy had a green Volkswagen.

Now, they had found Enough in the empty camp, bound and tied. And Walter had taken Enough from Frieda that morning. Ergo, it must have been Walter who stashed Enough in the camp. So, now where was Walter? Where was Peggy? Had they been here at the same time? A.E. had said Peggy had a phone call that morning. Who from? From Walter? Was Old Bill right? If money was the basis for all this killing and what seemed to be the total idiocy of moving Enough all over the mountain, where was the money? Who masterminded all this movement?

Of course. Hod nodded. It had started with Mr. Fremont and the cave. That's where the money had to be hidden. If the old minister had found it and the murderer had seen him returning to the lodge with it, that would be reason enough to kill.

The thing is, thought Hod, it's just too damn simple. It's right there all laid out for us. Somebody couldn't let us know their identity and couldn't let the booty be found. And it looks like it might have been Walter, for sure.

Now, where is he? He was here, Peggy was here. There must be a connection. Let's look for car tracks.

Within ten minutes Hod had located Walter's four-wheel drive well hidden with brush behind one of the camps.

Peggy's Volkswagen was not to be found.

Until Hod, following the tracks, decided it had to be in the lake. Stripping down, he swam directly out from the shore. Within minutes he'd located the little car. He dived to locate its driver.

Dick, watching from the shore, shook his head. "Not Peggy too."

"Nope." Hod shook the water out of his ears. "The door is open on the driver's side. No one in the car. If Peggy ever was, she's not there now. I tell you what I think. I don't think she's in the pond. I'm going to bet money she's out there, on that peninsula right now. Probably pretty waterlogged, but alive. Let's just take a look and see." And he started in toward shore.

A shivering Peggy Canevari, with one arm broken, was glad to have help. She had struggled with the door. It had been a long swim, underwater most of the way, and her courage had run out about the time she'd reached shore. She was face down when they found her, and she could barely speak when Dick gently pulled her up on the beach.

"He was going to kill me."

"Like as not he would have. I knew you had to be a better driver than to go in the lake by chance. The sad part of it is, I doubt you're going anyplace for a while. You knew, didn't you, it was Walter?"

"Yes." It was almost a whisper. "I didn't know at first, I didn't know he had anything to do with the murders until today. I didn't want to believe it. But when I found out what he'd done to Enough, I couldn't go away with him. And he was going to kill me. It just got worse and worse."

"Things get out of hand sometimes." Hod was still soaking wet, but he took the blanket Dick offered and wrapped it around the girl. "Enough's safe now. Motorboat just phoned from the hospital. And you're alive."

"I wish I had drowned." Peggy sobbed. "I just wish I had drowned."

CHAPTER THIRTY-THREE

Robbie saw no sign of movement on the edge of the woods again. Maybe it had been his imagination. Swampers had patience, they would wait for hours for game to pass. But today there was nothing moving in the place where he had been certain he'd seen the shadow of a presence.

"Come on, Howard, let's go. Got to find A.E." Robbie flicked the reins ever so slightly, and Howard moved forward, drawing the little blue cart with the baskets. Within another few minutes they had reached the lawn of the lodge. A.E. and Lee, sorting out paints in the kitchen, came out to greet them.

"Howard looks like he's happy drawing that cart, Robbie. It's made for him." Lee was delighted to see the pony again. "I'm almost sure he's a Pony of America."

Robbie nodded. "He's a good one. I don't want to have to lose him. I heard they thought he might belong to that man they found in the cache. But he doesn't want to go back to where he came from. They didn't treat him right. I want to keep him."

"We're going to try and see you do, Robbie." A.E. joined the conversation. "Just don't worry about it now. I'll see what can be worked out. He probably is valuable, but Dick'll help us find a way. Have you finally decided to sell those baskets?"

"Yup. Howard's going to need grain this winter. I'm going to have to get him more than one bale of hay. You said you could maybe help with selling, so I brought a few. Both kinds." He started to carefully unload the stacked baskets.

The Shermans came out on the porch, and Debby stepped forward and picked up one of the gathering baskets.

"How much is this?"

Robbie, faced with a real-world problem, turned to A.E. and Lee, who conferred on their first marketing decision.

"That one will go in the gallery for one hundred and fifty, Debby, but as it hasn't reached there yet, I believe one hundred would be fair. They are unique baskets, you'll never see any others like them. They're going to Boston."

Lee made some quick calculations, ignoring Robbie's surprised look.

"I'll take two, this one and that one." Debby reached forward into the cart. "Wait just a minute, and I'll go get my checkbook."

Behind Debby one of the new guests stepped off the porch and leaned over the side of the cart.

"Are they all for sale? I really like this one. I have a small gift shop, and I haven't seen any baskets of this caliber in some time. Do you suppose I could buy several and get a better price?"

Lee had found herself into marketing before she was really ready, but she was a business woman at heart and she knew Robbie had an unusual product.

"We intended these to go into a gallery in Boston, and I know about what they will sell for there. So there's no point in wholesaling them here. One hundred apiece here is the price and that is reasonable." Her voice was firm.

"Well, I'll take these three if I may. I'll go get a check."

Lee and A.E. looked at each other. "Maybe we ought to have a shop here. At least a few on display. Robbie, just unload what's left and I'll put them in the storeroom behind the kitchen. Wait a minute. I have to give you a receipt and the checks." A. E. felt a surge of warmth for the Swamper.

Robbie had stood quietly through the exchange, his hand on Howard's flank. Now he smiled one of his rare smiles and waved away the checks A.E. was about to put in his hand.

"No, you put the money away for me, A.E. I know I have to sign the checks, but I'm no good with banks. You do it for me, just so's I can ask you to get it out for me when I need it." Robbie's world stopped at the little country store in Bryant Pond. He had no desire to venture further into larger towns. School had been traumatic enough for Robbie. He depended on A.E. now for anything beyond the woods and the pond area.

A.E. agreed. The guests were still looking at the baskets as she made out a simple receipt for Robbie and showed him where to place his craftwork.

"Artwork, more like." Lee held up one basket longer than the rest, stained a deep brown. "Look at this, A. E. You could do a sketch of this. A still life."

"No, I've a better idea. Robbie, stay there." Hastily she gathered pencil and sketch pad from the pile in the corner of the kitchen. "I just need a few minutes. Just stay by Howard, Robbie. Right where you are now. Leave the baskets in the cart. No more selling now." She waved away the guests who still lingered.

Lee withdrew into the kitchen to make a fresh pot of coffee, stopping once to look through the window at the tall woman bent intently over her sketch pad.

This is her hour, her block of time. Perhaps she'll find her balance after all, thought Lee. Now if Hod can only find Enough and solve these murders I can go home and find my own solitude.

Dick took Peggy to the hospital emergency room to have her arm set. From there she would go to headquarters to be questioned. On the way over Rowe Hill Road the trooper let Hod out of the cruiser to walk down the road to Indian Pond.

Carrying his rifle and walking slowly, Hod was doing some heavy thinking as he looked from side to side.

"Must have been about here Walter took Enough from Frieda. Then he must have gone up 26, turned on 232, and doubled back to the north shore. Called up Peggy to join him, tied up Enough in the empty camp, and planned what he was going to do next. According to Peggy, they were to walk to Bethel and get his second car at his house, then drive by back roads up to Canada. I got to give him credit for being inventive. Not what we'd expect he'd do. Walking five miles wouldn't suit your average criminal. But then, Walter ain't average."

Hod's use of language varied according to setting. Standing now by the road, thinking the puzzle out, trying to get into Walter's mind, the woodsman surfaced, the hunter in his brain was tracking down the hunted.

So, now, next step, where was Walter? If Hod figured it right, when Peggy drove into the pond, Walter would have left the scene. He would have heard Dick's cruiser coming into the camps. No time to deal with Enough. So, Walter had to go into the woods. And having left his car hidden, he would need another car.

"Where would I go?" Hod walked along thinking aloud. A man who planned a five-mile walk to Bethel would try anything. He needed a car, and even though he thought Peggy had drowned, nevertheless she might have gotten out of the Volkswagen. That being the case, she could tell his plan to the law. So he would have to change his plan. No walk to Bethel. Find a car close by. And close by was the lodge.

Hod nodded his head. Yep, if it was me I'd change my plan. So now I'm looking for a car. The lodge it has to be. I'll go to the last place they'd think to look. Back over the mountain to Indian Lodge. Take the lower trail. Several cars there in the lodge parking lot, just wait until dark and take one. Bound to be keys in one, and if not, for sure A.E. leaves her keys in her old jeep every night, I'll bet. Once out of there I'll head north, find another car, walk if necessary and I'll make it. Not far to the border, and I'm free. Yep, thought Hod, he's going to do the last thing we figure he'd do.

Hod spoke aloud. "Takes a fox to catch a fox. And I intend to catch him."

Walter, now the subject of a new all points bulletin, had bedded down on the edge of the hardwood stand, just out of sight and protected by the fact that the yellow tape still remained along the side of the meadow. Robbie had been correct in seeing movement. At that moment Walter had been taking off his backpack. He settled into the back of a slash pile to wait for evening. He had packed important items into his small backpack while waiting for Peggy. Binoculars, extra clothing, chocolate, matches, space blanket, the usual survival kit most woodsmen, campers, and outdoorsmen keep on hand. Walter was a planner. Now his life and his freedom depended on how good a planner he turned out to be.

He'd not counted on Hod Cole. Lawmen thought from the hunter's point of view. Hod approached a puzzle differently.

Hod became the hunted.

He was rarely wrong.

CHAPTER THIRTY-FOUR

Now it was a waiting game.

Motorboat sat by Enough's bed in the hospital waiting for the IV's to do their job. In a day's time Enough would be his old self, smelling sweeter and ready to go back to work at the lodge. Motorboat would stay nearby during that time, just in case. The Kenworth could wait.

Peggy, arm in a cast, retreated to her small apartment after being interrogated by the sheriff's office. Although she had suspected, she had not really been sure of what Walter was doing, or was capable of doing. Saddened and chastised, she withdrew from everyone, even A.E., who would have welcomed her back at the lodge.

Lee took her vacation time to help A.E., who had to wait three days until a new kitchen maid and waitress could be hired. Nancy, Mr. Fremont's niece, arrived, and more guests were coming later in the week. Yet A.E. took her hour daily to sketch, and she had begun an oil of Robbie and the cart with its load of baskets.

She had taken her mortgage application (finished with Lee's assistance) to Indian Mountain Bank that Monday afternoon even though Walter was not there to greet her. No one at the bank knew the complete details, and a shaken staff was attempting to carry on as if Walter had simply gone off on a long vacation. How could it possibly be otherwise?

"I don't think there will be a problem on your loan." The mortgage officer was friendly. "We are so upset, Ms. Gibbons, about Mr. Desmond's disappearance. Nothing like that has ever happened at our bank. They do think he's no longer in the area, that's what I heard this morning. I can't believe Mr. Desmond was a drug connection."

Dick's answer came in detail from Massachusetts. There was no doubt that

Walter had been one of the biggest connecting links in the New England states. Dick and Hod finally pieced together the chain of events, but Walter remained missing. Theories abounded as to his whereabouts, but none were proven. So the law waited, convinced he was no longer in Maine or, at least, in the Bryant Pond area.

Frieda waited, feeling better. She no longer feared this birth. Dr. Anna instilled confidence. Dr. Anna, who had shared a jelly glass of Jack Daniels on Old Bill's cabin porch in the late afternoon. It was Old Bill himself who had initiated their friendship almost as though it was in memory of Alexander. He had driven his army jeep up to Bethel and marched into Dr. Anna's office, introduced himself, and found, as Alexander had, a kindred soul.

Only Hod questioned the wisdom of calling off the searchers. "I don't think he's out of the area," he said to Dick." I think he's right under our noses, hidden and waiting for something. And I believe that something is transportation. He's either waiting for somebody he's connected with, or he's waiting for a way out. My guess is a way out. He's decided not to walk out. So he needs a car.

Must be planning to steal one. No, Dick, I think he's still here."

"Well, you're the only one who thinks so. Couple of my men looked up in the cave, down on the trails. No signs of him anyplace. It's been two days now. I doubt he's around this area."

Hod, sitting on the porch of the lodge waiting to carry trash out for Lee from the kitchen, narrowed his eyes.

"Tell you what," he said. "I'm just going to wait."

Walter was patient. For the remainder of Monday he watched the lodge, thinking it was lucky that no one had thought to have Casco and Key hunt for him. One of their favorite tricks was to sniff him out of a hiding of more than a mile's distance. Carol must be back from Boston by now; the bank and the town must know he was missing. Carol might think of the dogs' trick.

No. Cotton fluff. She'd never think of it, just of the disgrace he had heaped on the family. He felt a pang. He would miss the dogs and the mare, but not his family. He was surprised at how little he would miss them.

Right now he had to be sharp. He had been watching the parking lot steadily, from an ideal vantage point, and sooner or later someone would leave the keys in their car. At first dusk he had crept up carefully, always keeping an object between himself and the lodge, never standing out in the open. Monday night was cloudy early on. Still, all of the cars were locked.

By Tuesday evening the sky was overcast and dark. No moon, no stars. There's a storm on its way for sure, thought Walter. A good time to drive. And, this night, one of the cars, a dark blue Ford, was unlocked. Wonder of wonders, with keys still there. The license plate showed Virginia, no doubt Mr. Fremont's niece. The old man had come back full circle.

Quietly, Walter drew back from the car and listened. Creeping slowly along the side of the building, staying in the shadow, he heard only the hum of the old-fashioned refrigerator in the kitchen area. He needed now only to return to his hiding place in the hardwood stand, gather up his backpack and the money, removed from the coffee can but still in its oilskin wrapping.

If any of the guests heard the car start and drive off they would not think twice— this was a lodge, after all, and people came in and out at all hours. The car would not be missed until morning.

Walter crept slowly through the meadow, past the fence and to his hiding place. The wind was rising now, moaning a little as it swept down the mountainside, flicking the tops of trees, scattering the first fallen leaves and rippling the surface of the pond. A moaning sound, spiritual. Maybe it was the mountain. The mountain protesting the killings.

Backpack on his shoulders now, Walter kept low and to one side of the meadow. It was a night for goblins, and he felt his way carefully, trying not to lose the path. Ahead he could see the light in the lodge that A.E. always left on. He used that light as a guide.

Only now, it moved.

Walter stood still.

It moved again.

Impossible, he said to himself. He had seen the table lamp on, inside the great room, when he'd peeked in one of the windows. It was an old-fashioned brass lamp with glass shade, set on one of the rustic tables against a window, left on at night in case one of the guests had to come downstairs to find something left behind. A.E. had long ago decided to leave this light on all night, as guests tended to wake her up for forgotten purses or scarves.

Table lamps don't move. It seemed to be coming nearer, over the lawn, heading toward the meadow.

Walter stood very still. And, at that moment the barred owl called to its mate. Hoohoo-hoohoo-hoohoo-hoohooaw.

And something, something was coming toward him.

For the first time Walter panicked. He had thought it all out, gambled when necessary, planned for another life, and now, in this last moment, he panicked.

He turned and ran.

And forgot about the beehives.

A.E. heard screaming. Men's voices, shouting. There was the sound of feet running. Looking out, she saw lights in the meadow. She dressed hurriedly and ran down the stairs to open the door. She saw the rotating lights of a police cruiser and heard Dick yelling, "Hod, you O.K.?"

And the answer, "A couple of stings but they got him. Keep everybody away. You better call an ambulance. Send for Robbie, he'll know what to do. Those bees are one mad bunch."

CHAPTER THIRTY-FIVE

"They're snarky, don't like being disturbed this time of year. Got their honey all put by and don't like anyone tippin' over the hive. There's bees from all over out there. Come to join in eating the honey. Frames and supers all over. They'll stay with it, but I got to wait a bit till they settle to get them back in."

Robbie had been picked up by A.E. and sat, at five o'clock on Wednesday morning, in the lodge kitchen sipping coffee.

The sheriff's men had come and gone. Walter, badly stung, had been transported to the hospital by ambulance. He would be under heavy guard until he was well enough to go to jail. A.E. and Robbie sat alone in the kitchen.

"Why'd he do it, A.E.?" Robbie accepted a muffin.

"Money, Robbie. Such a waste. I don't know about the man in the cache, Manny Watrous. But Mr. Fremont was a good man. And Enough nearly died. All because of the money Walter had hidden, according to what Hod said. All that money. And now Walter'll spend the rest of his life in jail."

Robbie was thoughtful. "Never thought money was much."

A.E. laughed. "Only for exchange, Robbie. Only for what you can exchange it for that you need. Like your baskets. You sell one and you have feed for Howard. That's all I want it for, Robbie. Just to fix up the lodge a little, and paint every day. It'll be sunrise soon. Hadn't you better get at those bees?"

Robbie nodded, zipping up the suit and adjusting his head net. Taking his equipment, he set out across the lawn. A.E., coffee cup in hand, climbed the stairs to the tower room. She stood in front of the oil taking shape on the easel by the north window. Robbie, Howard, the blue cart with its load of gathering baskets.

"I can do it," she whispered. "I can really paint. The next one will be Motorboat fishing from the birchbark canoe. Maybe there's a spot for me in a Boston gallery."

Lee had put a paste of baking soda on Hod's bee stings, but his face was still partially swollen. Five o'clock on this Wednesday morning, as A.E. talked with Robbie, Dick and Motorboat had arrived at the farm from the sheriff's office. The ever present coffeepot sat in the the middle of the pine kitchen table. Beside it rested the head light Hod had worn the night before. Walter's nemesis.

Lee poured into thick china mugs and handed them to the men. She passed slices of cranberry bread.

"How about scrambled eggs and bacon?" She smiled as they nodded their heads. She put out milk and sugar for Dick, who sat with his hat shoved back on his head and his tie loosened.

"Well, it all fits together, far as we can make out. Walter was the connection. He actually didn't intend to kill Mr. Fremont, figured a blow to the head would just knock him out and he'd drop the can. Walter'd come up to the cave to remove the money, when he saw the minister leaving to go back down the path to the lodge. He also saw Robbie sleeping on the ledge below him. The mallet handle stuck out of the pack basket, and Walter just grabbed it. He said it all happened fast. He shadowed Mr. Fremont and had to make his move before they got out into the meadow. He gave him a good whack and got the can, went back up the trail, and put the mallet back in the pack basket again. Couldn't plan anything like that in a million years. Walter said it just happened.

"Then he took the can back and buried it in his garden. Nothing unusual to see Walter running or jogging every morning. He did it all the time—nobody's going to think anything was out of order. He was all over that mountain, night and day. That night A.E. saw a light it was him back up at the cave. He kept moving the can back and forth, afraid the woodchucks would dig it up in his garden and afraid we might search the cave again. He had a small pair of binoculars he carried with him. That's how he saw Enough, and he wasn't sure how much Enough had seen. Walter thought he might have seen the attack on Mr. Fremont. So, he had his eyes on Enough from the beginning. When he found him at the stone cache, he decided he had to get rid of him. Walter took off the bandanna he wore for a sweat band, tied it around Enough's eyes. Then he took off his sweat socks and gagged the boy's mouth and tied his hands. He was sure inventive." Dick paused.

"See, that's where we went wrong. We thought it was all planned. Wasn't at all. Just spur of the moment. Did it that way from the beginning when he met Manny Watrous and told him he wanted out. When Manny threatened him, Walter didn't hesitate. The pony spooked and ran away."

"I wondered about Howard." Lee leaned forward, her elbows on the table.

"By the time Walter came back to see if he could find the pony, he had disappeared. Robbie had rescued him."

"What do you suppose Walter would have done if he'd found Howard." Lee was anxious.

"Probably killed him too."

"Did Peggy know?" Lee put her hand gently on Hod's shoulder.

"No, I don't think so. She says she suspected, but she didn't want to believe it. Walter was a way out for her, and although she felt bad for his family she didn't think he'd commit murder. She knew he was a drug connection, that's where the money came from, but she wouldn't allow herself to entertain more thoughts. Until Enough came up missing, and then, when she knew, as everyone did, that he was supposed to take Enough to the hospital after he met Frieda. Then Peggy knew."

Hod nodded. "She said she didn't really care whether she escaped from the Volkswagen. She knew Walter would kill her, too, so she took a long chance."

"Only one thing good came out of the whole sordid mess." Lee spoke out after a long pause.

"What?" Dick was bushed, and ready to go home to Frieda.

Lee smiled. "Howard. He'll spend the rest of his days with Robbie. And don't you ever go looking for that saddle."

EPILOGUE

Indian summer arrived in late October. Geese flew their age-old flyways to the south, and the sun shone beneficently on Indian Pond.

In a small bungalow in town, Frieda and Dick stood over a crib, admiring the eight-pound son they had just brought home from the hospital. Dr. Anna had been right. It had been an easy delivery and the baby was healthy and strong. This was a quiet moment for two people who had spent nearly nine months in turmoil. A new life to be grateful for—a new beginning.

On the porch of Old Bill's camp, Dr. Anna joined Bill in the last drink of the season. There was little conversation. There would be a another summer, God willing. Another jelly glass of Jack Daniels. Perhaps a new beginning for them. Silently they raised the glasses to each other, and to Alexander.

A.E.'s hands no longer shook. Dr. Anna had diagnosed her problem as a genetic one, familial tremor. This could be controlled by medication and, for the first time in a long while, A.E. felt in control. Today she was finishing an oil of Motorboat, who was fishing on the pond in the birchbark canoe. Only the flick of his line entering the surface of the water could be heard; the shadows from trees overhanging the shore were telling her it was time to stop and call him in. There was a silent understanding between them now, colored by the happenings at the lodge and their mutual caring for Enough.

Enough—one of whose first questions after getting out of the hospital was "When are we going to the New Hampshire Speedway?"

And Motorboat had gone right out and bought two tickets for the big race next July.

A.E. smiled silently, thinking of this. She collected her paints and brushes. Dinnertime now. She had a new kitchen helper, but Peggy was missed. Peggy, who had faded out of their lives and gone to another state.

Maybe next year she would close the lodge. The first painting, the one of Robbie and Howard and the cart full of baskets, had been exhibited along with the baskets in a Boston gallery. The baskets sold within weeks at about the price Lee and A.E. had hoped. The surprise was that A.E.'s painting sold for a record price to a collector of American contemporary art. A new beginning.

Several miles away, in the late afternoon sunshine, Lee and Hod planted daffodil bulbs alongside a small gravestone on an island in the Androscoggin. Lee's hands set the bulbs firmly in the holes Hod had scooped in the unyielding earth. The man and woman did not speak. They had shared a simple lunch on the moss under the tall pines. Then Lee had brought out the small sack of daffodil bulbs she had been keeping for this moment. There had been little conversation but a quiet understanding. Hod's head was bowed as he dug with the small spade Lee kept in the car for liberating (as she called it) any wild plants she took a fancy to bring home to the garden.

"There. They will be beautiful in the spring, Hod." Lee smoothed the dirt, placing a bit of green moss on top to take away the sight of raw earth.

They rose, gathered the picnic basket and thermos, and walked slowly to the car. A new beginning.

And, up on the ledges, far above Indian Pond, Robbie sat, scanning the gray-green tapestry of the valley below. A scent of woodsmoke rose from the chimney of the lodge. The smell of Indian summer was on the land.

A Robbie who was no longer alone. In truth, he was King of the Mountain at last.

The last of the Swampers, the owner of Howard, and Lord of all he surveyed.